For the women who want to get railed by the villain.

And also redeem him.

REDEMPTION

A DARK STALKER ROMANCE

FAVORITE MALADY
BOOK 2

JULIA SYKES

Cover Design: Jaqueline Kropmanns - Design

Editing: Rebecca Cartee

AUTHOR'S NOTE

This is a deeply personal book for me, and it's been a cathartic way to process trauma. However, I never want to upset someone who might find the themes disturbing. Please check my website for more information, and be gentle with yourself.

julia-sykes.com

1

ABIGAIL

I wake up to a nightmare.

In the second between unconsciousness and waking, I believe that the awful scene with Dane was just that: a nightmare.

But then I realize that I can't move my limbs, and something soft is wedged between my teeth. The makeshift gag presses deep into my mouth, and part of my brain registers that it's one of Dane's neckties.

More silken material binds my wrists and ankles. They're drawn together at the small of my back, stretching my body in a hogtied position. I'm completely helpless to do anything but writhe on my side.

Fear crashes into me like the sharp slap of an icy

ocean wave in January. Terror rips from my chest in a primal scream, but it's muffled by the knotted gag.

Dane shushes me gently, and I shudder in horror at the shadow of comfort that tempts me.

The man I love is the masked man who attacked me.

He's my online confidante, GentAnon.

He has scores of my paintings hanging in this house, the house across the street from my apartment building.

How long has he been watching me?

My mind races through all the times I felt shivery and trembled in his presence, even on our early dates. The images flicker in a nauseating film reel. Even then, my body recognized the predator. But I'm addicted to the fear, the threat.

He learned all of my darkest secrets, and he used them against me.

The mattress dips beside me, and my dark god appears in my line of vision, blocking out the view of my paintings.

We're still in the bedroom of the powder blue house, in the horrific shrine to me.

I can't have been out for very long. He caught me in a chokehold, but I don't feel bruises around my neck.

Dane wouldn't risk damaging his pet.

My stomach churns, and I taste acid on the back of my tongue.

Another scream tears from my soul—pure horror this time. Despair. Denial.

Dane's familiar, elegant hand is achingly gentle as he strokes my hair back from my cheek. His eyes are deep green pools, and fine lines sharpen his heartbreaking features.

"Hush now, pet. I'm not going to hurt you."

I shudder and cringe away, but I can't move more than an inch in my bound state. He has no trouble keeping me within his tender reach, and he caresses my cheek as though to prove my powerlessness.

"I didn't want it to be this way." His cultured voice is deep with something like regret.

The slightly rough tone threads confusion through my panicked, racing thoughts.

I don't know what's real anymore. Is he my protective, fierce lover? Or is he a heartless, calculating monster?

The memory of the woolen skull mask in my fingers is all too sharp.

I definitely didn't dream that.

"I can't let you go to the police," he reasons. He's

unnervingly calm, and I recognize his bedside manner voice.

My vision blurs as tears surge. I desperately blink them away so that I can keep the threat in sight.

His thumb traces the line of my cheekbone as he wipes away the wetness on my cheeks.

My entire body goes cold, and a violent shiver makes my bound limbs quake.

"Don't be afraid," he soothes over the sound of my muffled pleas.

Let me go, I try to beg. *You don't have to do this.*

But the words are garbled behind the gag, and my assailant seems unfazed by my distress. He's still touching me as though he intends to comfort me, but he's coolly composed. I recognize the merciless, flat expression that sets his handsome face in stony planes. It used to make me tremble with desire. Now, I shudder in pure terror.

"Try not to struggle," he says, a gentle command. "You'll only strain your muscles. I have to go to my place to get a few things, but you'll be safe here."

He gestures in the direction of the nightstand. My phone is propped up against a lamp, the camera directed at me.

"I'll have you on video call the whole time." He says it like a reassurance. "I wouldn't leave you alone like this if I didn't absolutely have to. I'll watch over you, even when I'm not here."

Ice encases my bones. How long has he been doing just that: *watching over me?*

He twirls my purple curl around his finger before withdrawing regretfully. "I'll be back soon."

He stands and starts walking away.

Please! I scream into the gag. *Dane!*

He seems to recognize his name, because he flinches like I flung a knife that hit its mark deep in his chest. Then he shrugs and strides out of the bedroom, disappearing into the living room. I hear the front door open, then close. The lock engages.

I scream for help, for mercy, for salvation.

But no one hears my smothered pleas.

No one comes to save me.

~

I'M NOT sure how much time passes, but my muscles ache and my throat is sore by the time Dane returns.

He's holding a large, leather duffel bag in one hand. My passport is in the other.

My stomach drops, and I jerk against my restraints.

Why does he have my passport? How did he even get it?

I keep it in my nightstand drawer, and I locked my apartment door when...

My heart sinks as the awful reality of my situation weighs on my chest like a lead weight. Of course, Dane is able to easily access my apartment; he's the masked man. He's already been able to break in far too easily.

His sensual lips press together in a grim line as he sets the bag down and rummages in it for a few seconds.

My head starts swinging back and forth in horrified denial when I see the syringe he's holding.

"I had to get this from work," he explains, calm and cool. "It won't hurt."

He sits beside me and uncaps the needle. I writhe in a frenzy—prey caught in a trap.

One hand settles at my nape, pinning me with a firm but careful grip.

"Just a little pinch," he says, voice soft in that bedside manner.

I barely feel the needle slide into my neck, which only makes the horror of the drugs oozing into my system that much more potent. I shriek and jerk in his hold, but he might as well have a collar around my throat.

My limbs grow heavy, and darkness creeps in at the edges of my vision.

That featherlight touch on my hair again, petting me in a soothing rhythm.

"There's no point fighting it, Abigail," he admonishes. "The journey home will be much easier this way."

Easier for who? I want to rail, but my tongue is thick against the gag.

He's taking me somewhere, and I suspect that he doesn't mean my apartment when he says "home".

He has my passport.

We're going...

He's taking me...

I'm scared...

Even my disjointed thoughts float away, and his green eyes are the last thing I see before the darkness closes in.

2

DANE

Three Months Ago

The stunning woman at the bar has a quirky purple streak in her hair and a striking freckle on her right cheekbone. It's large enough that it's visible even at a distance. In my line of work, patients have asked me to remove smaller blemishes, but the longer I look at her, the more I think that it suits her. The mark makes her unique, and I admire the fact that she wears it with pride. She hasn't made an effort to conceal it with makeup.

Her posture is perfect, but her eyes stray to the

floor even when she's speaking to her friends. The dichotomy intrigues me. She's shy, but her bearing indicates confidence.

A man approaches her where she's swaying her hips near the bar. She can't seem to fully stop dancing even while she's waiting in the queue to order her drink.

The man steps into her personal space without invitation and leans in close to speak in her ear, presumably under the guise of being heard over the Latin music.

She stops swaying in her gentle dance, and her willowy body goes stiff.

The bastard doesn't seem to notice her obvious discomfort.

I'm prowling toward him before I realize what I'm doing.

"Dane?" I hear my associate, Meadows, call after me, but I wave him off.

He's known me long enough that he won't be offended by the dismissal; he's never gotten in the way of a conquest before.

I'm with her in seconds, and the creep is still far too close to her. My hand closes around his shoulder, and I drag him away from her. My grip is firm enough that the threat of violence is clear, but I don't toss him to the ground like I want to. I'm not sure how she would react to that, and I don't want to scare the woman who's captured my full attention.

And I don't want to get into a bar fight on my first night in Charleston. That wouldn't reflect well on my new practice with Meadows. He has social connections in the area, and I can't afford for word to get out that I'm dangerous.

The man who was harassing her tenses in my grip and whirls to face me. His fists clench, but before he can raise them, his eyes meet mine.

I don't bother to hide the monster within. I let him see exactly how cold and unfeeling I am—hurting him means absolutely nothing to me. I could destroy him without a second thought.

One of the advantages of lacking the impulse for empathy.

"She doesn't want to talk to you," I say smoothly, looming over the smaller man. "You should go."

It's not a suggestion; it's a threat.

He's in between me and my pretty prey, and I won't tolerate his presence for another second.

He's smart enough to get the hell out of my way before I force him to move. He swallows hard, and his shoulders dip in submission as he slinks off onto the crowded dance floor.

"Thanks," she says, her voice so shy and soft that I barely hear her over the music. Her eyes drop to the sticky floor. "You didn't have to do that."

"He was harassing you," I reply smoothly. "I absolutely did have to do that."

I decide not to tell her that I simply wanted to do it. Because he was a nuisance, and I want to talk to her. And he was making her uncomfortable.

Over the years, I've found that women like to feel protected.

Her cautious eyes lift to meet mine, and I'm momentarily stunned at their clear, aquamarine hue.

"Thank you," she says again, and this time, she doesn't glance away.

It takes all of my willpower to stop myself from closing the short distance between us so that she'll tip her head back and offer those rosebud lips to me.

I'm not a single-minded fool like the idiot who invaded her personal space.

I'm a careful monster, the perfect predator.

And I always capture my prey.

Judging by the way her lovely eyes are studying my face, I already have her interest. Women have always found me attractive, so this part is easy enough.

"You don't have to thank me," I say smoothly. "But you can let me buy you a drink."

Her delicately arched brows draw together. "You want to buy me a drink?"

I allow an indulgent smile to tilt my lips, even though I'm slightly irked that she seems the tiniest bit hesitant to accept. "I do."

She presses those pretty lips together, considering me for a second. Her clear-eyed gaze pins me with discomfiting intensity, and I find myself looking to the bartender to catch his attention.

I choose to ignore the odd moment.

When the bartender meets my eye, I place our order. "Another whiskey and a cosmopolitan."

The whiskey here is cheap, but I can't stomach the thought of masking the acrid flavor with a soft drink. My lovely companion, on the other hand, has sipped two pink cocktails in the last hour. It's not difficult to guess that she wants something sugary.

"Oh," she says. "I was drinking the slushies." She gestures at the machine filled with an icy pink drink at the back of the bar. There's a sign advertising two for ten dollars. "I can pay for mine."

I suppress a frown at her resistance. Instead, I arrange my features into my most charming smile.

The cosmopolitan appears on the bar before me.

"I'm not going to drink this. It'd be a shame for it to go to waste."

Proving my point, I take a sip of my whiskey, refusing to touch the sickly-sweet concoction.

She eyes me warily, and I choose to wait her out, quirking an expectant eyebrow.

"Okay." She sighs and reaches for the drink. "Thank you."

"What's your name?" I ask.

"Abigail. But everyone calls me Abby."

I don't want to be *everyone* to this woman. I want her to feel special. Desired.

She's strangely hesitant to succumb to my charms. My smile sharpens slightly. It's been a long time since I've been presented with a proper challenge.

"I'm Dane. Enjoy your drink, Abigail," I reply, savoring the flavor of her name on my tongue.

She lifts the frosted glass and takes a sip, as though she's complying without fully thinking through her actions.

Submissive.

Perfect.

As soon as she tastes the cocktail, her remarkable eyes practically roll back in bliss. They remain closed for a second, as though she's experiencing ecstasy at the sugar hit.

Hunger tightens my gut. She's definitely shy, but she's completely guileless. Her rapturous expression holds nothing back.

Her broad grin hits me square in the chest.

"This is *so good.*"

Fuck, the way she lingers over the words makes it sound like she could orgasm from her sensory response to nothing more than a sweet drink.

She'll sound beautiful when she screams my name in bed.

"I'm glad you like it," I say, half a heartbeat later than I should.

Something about this woman challenges my usual composure. I can't predict her actions, and she doesn't easily fall into my seductive games.

She almost refused my offer to buy her a drink, but then she submitted when I used a firmer tone with her.

I'm intrigued.

She's beautiful, but that's not what attracts me to her. As a plastic surgeon, I see beautiful women every day, and they come to me to make them even more physically perfect.

With her enchanting freckle and understated but lovely lips, Abigail isn't perfect.

But she might just be the most enticing woman I've ever met, and I've only spoken to her for a few minutes.

"Where are you from?" she asks. "I like your accent."

My chest warms at the first admission of her attraction to me, and my smile tilts into a smirk. Her gaze fixes on my mouth.

She's just as intrigued as I am.

"England," I reply. "But I've lived in the States for a while now. Are you from Charleston? I'm new here."

I like her accent too. There's a soft Southern drawl that makes her words almost breathy, but it's subtle enough to not be a distraction. I want to hear her panting and begging in my bed in that sultry voice.

She takes another sip of her drink, as though she can't resist sampling the sweetness on her tongue.

"I grew up around here," she says. "And I've lived in Charleston since college. It's such a beautiful city. I'm sure you'll love it here."

"Yes," I agree, allowing my gaze to flick over her face in obvious appreciation. "Beautiful."

A pretty shade of pink flushes her cheeks, and she takes a bigger gulp of her drink.

I'm starting to find her shyness charming. Will she blush when I lean in close and whisper all the filthy things I want to do to her?

Resolutely, I maintain a respectful distance between us. My prey isn't ready to be cornered. She strikes me as a soft-spoken, sweet Southern belle. Judging by her perfect posture, she's probably a good girl, well-behaved. She'll be scandalized by my perverted plans for her, but I'm confident that I can bend her to my will.

I've never failed to seduce a conquest before. She'll accept my darker games by the end of the night, and I'll show her greater ecstasy than she ever thought possible. I just have to handle her carefully.

"Have you been to Battery Park yet?" Her voice is a touch higher now as she struggles to make small talk when I'm practically burning her with my intense gaze.

I should probably soften that intensity, but I'm enjoying the edgy energy crackling between us too much to rein myself in. She sways toward me ever so slightly, drawn in by the threat lurking behind my cocky smirk.

"I haven't been to the park yet. I only arrived in town a few days ago. You can show me around."

I let my mask slip a bit further, and my smile sharpens. I keep her pinned in my steady, unwavering stare, and her lips part slightly on a panting intake of breath.

She drops her gaze and drains the last inch of her drink, as though she needs the cool liquid to soothe her flushed skin.

"What brought you to Charleston?" she counters instead of immediately agreeing to be my tour guide.

I smother a small frown at her renewed resistance. The chemistry we share is undeniable, electric. But perhaps it's potent enough to make her uncomfortable. I must be right about her: she's a good girl.

I recall the way she stiffened when the creep invaded her personal space. Maybe she doesn't often flirt with men.

"I came here for work," I say simply.

I don't care to talk about my job; it doesn't define me. I'll never understand the American fixation on career as a defining characteristic. It's just a way to make money and afford the lifestyle I desire.

Before she can press for more information, I flag

down the bartender and order her another cosmopolitan.

"I can get it," she says quickly, reaching into her purse.

I pay with my black card before she can fully pull out a wad of one-dollar bills.

Interesting. She's scraping money together to pay for her drinks, but she doesn't want me to take care of her.

Out of pride?

I shake off my curiosity. Her reasons don't matter; she won't pay for another drink tonight. She will have to accept that.

Women usually love being taken care of. This isn't the first time I've engaged in this little game where a woman reaches for her purse. But it is the first time that I truly believe she's uncomfortable with me paying. It's confounding, especially considering her meager funds.

I have plenty of money, and I want to spend it on her.

"I've got it." I deepen my tone again, brooking no resistance as I press the cocktail glass into her hand.

Her slender fingers close around it without further protest.

Definitely submissive.

She takes another long draw of her sweet drink, a sign of nervousness that I savor even as I worry that she might be drinking too fast. With her slender frame, I'd be surprised if she can handle much alcohol.

"You should check out Folly Beach sometime," she says, making more small talk to soothe her nerves. She's painstakingly polite, and she seems almost conditioned to continue the conversation.

Definitely a good Carolina girl.

I'll enjoy corrupting her later.

But for now, she won't drink more. I have no interest in taking a drunk woman home with me.

I want her fully aware of every moment we share, every drop of pleasure I wring from her delicate body.

"I'd love to go to the beach with you sometime," I say, maintaining my assertion that she'll show me around the area.

It's strange that I'm setting a date with a woman I barely know. Usually, a night or two is enough to sate my physical needs.

But I definitely wouldn't mind spending more time in Abigail's company. She's a puzzle I haven't quite figured out, and I won't let her go until I solve it.

I reach out and pluck the half-empty cocktail glass from her hand before setting it on the bar alongside my whiskey.

"Dance with me." It's a command, and she doesn't pull away when I take her dainty hand in mine.

"But we haven't finished our drinks," she protests, even as she allows me to lead her away from the bar.

"I've had enough to drink," I counter smoothly, choosing not to chastise her for gulping her cocktails.

It seemed to be an anxious response, and I don't want to rebuke her for being nervous around me. I like keeping her on edge.

"I'm not a very good dancer," she equivocates when we step onto the dance floor.

"Let me lead," I command. "Take my hands."

I grasp both of her smaller hands in mine before she can make the choice herself, caging her slender fingers in a careful but firm grip.

"Hold on to me."

I step toward her, and she eases back in perfect time. I'm not sure if she's following me in the dance or if she's edging away from my predatory energy.

I pull her into me, spinning her around so that

she twirls before her back presses against my chest. Her shocked laugh is melodic, twining through the beat of the music. I keep her trapped against me with an arm around her waist for a few swaying steps. She moves with me beautifully, surrendering to my control despite her nerves.

I spin her away before she can get uncomfortable in my arms, and she laughs again. She tosses her glossy, sable hair, and the golden lights catch on the pretty purple curl that falls over her left shoulder. I crave to twine it around my fist and pull her in for a fierce kiss.

Instead, I spend the next two songs twirling her around the dance floor. Her cheeks are an even deeper shade of pink, and her lips part on little panting breaths as her body warms for me.

Desire pulses through my veins, and it's all I can do to keep my hands from straying to her pert ass instead of gripping her waist.

Hunger for this woman sets my teeth on edge, but I'm enjoying the new, slightly discomfiting sensation. I'm losing myself in the hunt: a more savage psychological dance as I lure her in with every step. Our bodies move in time, and I allow her to see my need for her burning through my eyes. We'll be perfectly compatible when we fuck in a few short hours. Abigail is proving that she naturally follows my lead, and despite her good girl sensibilities, she'll succumb to my dark needs.

The music slows to something more sensual, and I tug her flush with my chest. My arm is an iron band around her lower back, pinning her to me as I methodically back her off the dancefloor with each swaying step.

We reach a quieter, shadowy corner of the bar, and her eyes flare the moment she realizes that I have her trapped.

But she doesn't stiffen in distaste like she did when the uncouth idiot invaded her space at the bar earlier.

Her head tips back. Her pupils are dilated, and the lights flash over her eyes so that they shine like precious gemstones.

I finally indulge myself and twine her amethyst curl around my finger. Her hair is like silk, and I wonder how soft her skin will feel against mine.

I lean in slowly, and her head drops back farther. I allow her to simmer in anticipation, until she's practically trembling with need.

At the last moment, I tilt my face to the side so that my cheek skims over hers. My lips tease the shell of her ear when I whisper, "What does a good Carolina girl like you want me to do to her?"

I'm testing her, teasing her. I'll deny her the kiss she so clearly desires until she yields a bit. I want to know a sensual secret so that I can better manipulate her into accepting my twisted games.

"Who says I'm a good girl?" she breathes, and the words are hot against my skin.

My fine hairs stand on end, a strange prickling sensation on the back of my neck that I've never felt before.

I hum in consideration, and she shivers in response to the low rumble. I breathe in her sweet, slightly fruity scent and indulge myself, nuzzling her silken hair.

"What if I tell you to be a good girl for me?"

Her breath catches, but she shakes her head. "I'm not good."

Boldly, I shift my tender touch on her hair so that I can capture her nape in my hand. "I can make you be my good girl. Would you like that, Abigail?"

"Make me?" It's barely audible, a little puff of warm air on my cheek.

"You'll love being my good girl," I promise darkly, and she quivers in my hold. "I guarantee it."

I graze my teeth over her vulnerable artery. "Tell me what you want."

"I…" She trails off, so I give her a small bite to loosen her tongue with a little flare of warning pain. "I want you to make me," she whispers in a rush. "I want you to pin me down and use me."

Fuck. I swallow the curse and breathe through the pulse of lust that surges through my body. My cock stiffens, and I wrestle for control so that I don't get a hard-on in public.

"Will you struggle?" My voice is rougher now, crueler.

Her lips brush my cheek as she asks breathily, "Do you want me to?"

I bite back a groan. This woman is maddeningly perfect. I need to drive into her wet heat and fuck her hard until she weeps for mercy.

I've never unleashed my savage side before. I've always been careful to hide the cruelest parts of my nature behind cool control in the bedroom. I manipulate and seduce to get what I want, but I'm never fully myself.

The prospect of letting my mask drop entirely tempts me to the edge of sanity.

I grit my teeth and barely restrain myself from

shoving her against the wall to claim her mouth with all the ruthlessness I'm capable of.

Not here.

I can't let anyone see me like that.

Expect maybe *her.*

The sensual promise of this darkest game makes my blood burn in my veins. My fingers tighten around her nape, and I drag her closer. I nip at the sensitive spot beneath her ear, and she releases the most erotic little whimper I've ever heard.

She wants this. She wants *me.*

The real, unmasked version of me that I've never shown anyone.

This is dangerous. Reckless.

I don't know Abigail at all, and I'm considering a rash act that's completely out of character for me.

"Abby!" A masculine voice calls out from behind me, tearing the moment I'm sharing with my pretty prey.

She jerks in my hold, and for a moment, I firm my grip on her slender neck. She draws in a sharp breath and softens against me, melting into the harsh touch.

So fucking perfect.

"Abby." The man says again. "I can't find Stacy. She's not answering my calls."

I round on him, fixing him with a glower like he's a fly I'll swat away without a second thought.

He pales slightly, and his mouth drops open on a gasp beneath his neat black moustache.

Fuck.

I struggle to summon up my civilized mask again. This person is clearly Abigail's friend, and he's concerned for another woman they know. I can't eviscerate him for daring to interrupt us.

"Franklin?" Her voice slurs slightly on his name when she returns to a normal speaking volume. I hadn't noticed the slower cadence to her speech when we'd been whispering forbidden secrets.

Is she drunk?

I recall the fact that she drank at least two slushies before I plied her with one and a half cosmopolitans. How much of a lightweight is she? Did she have even more slushies before I arrived at the bar?

I'd been concerned about allowing her to drink her second cocktail, but maybe she's already had too much.

I force myself to put distance between us so that her friend, Franklin, can talk to her.

She stumbles away from the wall as soon as I stop pinning her.

I rake a hand through my hair, strangely agitated.

"Where's Stacy?" she asks, and her eyes are slightly unfocused as she squints at the crowd of people swaying on the dancefloor.

Franklin sighs and rolls his eyes. "Not you, too, Abby. Come on, I'll get you home before you stumble off with some hottie." He wraps a supportive arm around her shoulders and starts to steer her away.

She sways into him, and it takes all my willpower to stop myself from tearing her friend away from her.

She clearly needs the support, and I'm a stranger to her.

The stranger who plied her with alcohol and then cornered her at the bar. I practically groped her in public.

No wonder her friend is considering me through narrowed eyes. I must seem like a predator to him.

I am a predator, but not in the way he thinks. The idea of claiming Abigail when she's inebriated leaves me cold. I want her fully aware of every moment we share. And I don't want her to experience an ounce of regret in the morning.

So, I fold my arms over my chest and remain

rooted to the spot while I watch him steer her toward the exit.

"Is Stacy okay?" I hear her ask. She's speaking unnecessarily loudly; she's clearly lost her volume control.

"I don't know." Franklin is exasperated.

"We can't leave her," Abigail insists.

"She already left. We can call..." Their conversation is lost beneath the pulsing music, and I'm left standing in the corner like a granite statue.

My teeth are locked hard enough to make my jaw ache, but I have to remain resolutely still to prevent myself from going after her.

A mad idea sparks.

I can't let her slip away.

I need to know this woman, and I won't give up so easily.

My coiled muscles relax, and I saunter after her, keeping a dozen revelers between us to conceal the fact that I'm following her.

I didn't even get her number. I can't openly pursue her now without drawing negative attention from Franklin. He's clearly protective, and I don't want him to try to stop me from getting to my prey.

It would be unfortunate if I had to hurt her friend.

That would complicate my plans to seduce her.

I follow them out into the night, trailing her until she disappears into a dilapidated apartment building.

When I'm reassured that Franklin isn't in her apartment—I can see her clearly through her window that provides a view into her living room—I stroll away from her.

I know where she lives now. I can come back in the morning.

I'll find a way to conveniently meet her again. Charleston isn't a big city, and it won't seem too strange for us to see each other coincidentally.

She won't know that our second meeting will be by my design.

I'll have Abigail in my bed, and I'll learn her darkest secrets. She will surrender, and then this strange, clawing need that's assailing me will abate.

3

ABIGAIL

Now

I waver in and out of consciousness, completely disoriented. I'm only semi-lucid for a few minutes at a time before I feel the prick of the needle, and the world dissolves again.

Dane is placing me in a plush seat and buckling me in. The floor tilts, and I dimly register the sound of a plane taking off. One big hand rests against the side of my head, gently urging me to lean on his shoulder. My eyelids droop, and I breathe in his spicy cedarwood scent as I float away.

DANE'S strong hands are on me, lifting me as though I'm a doll. Then I'm seated again, but the world is sliding past me. Or I'm rolling forward. My head swims, so I close my eyes and drift.

"ABIGAIL IS MY PATIENT." I register Dane's accent, smooth and cultured as ever. "The flight was difficult for her after the procedure, so I gave her something to help manage the pain. I have her passport here."

My eyes flutter open, and I squint against harsh, sterile light. The uniformed officer looms over me, and I realize I'm still seated.

The man doubles in my blurred vision. He's looking down at the two passports on the desk between us.

Something heavy settles on my shoulder: Dane's hand. A reassurance? Or a warning?

Distant fear twists my belly, a fleeting twinge.

The officer glances up at Dane, then nods deferentially. "Welcome home, Lord Graham."

"My father is Lord Graham," Dane says smoothly, all charm and self-deprecating grace. "I'm just Dane."

The officer glances at me. "You're in good hands, miss. Get well soon."

A soft whimper catches in my throat. I don't understand what's happening or where I am, and my chest is getting too tight to draw in full breaths.

"It's all right," Dane soothes as the world starts to roll by me again. "We'll get you more meds as soon as we're out of the airport."

The rolling sensation makes my stomach turn. I close my eyes to hold back my rising nausea.

I barely feel the needle sliding into my neck, and then everything is warm and dark.

Dane's massive body cradles mine, and his unique, masculine scent enfolds me. I breathe him in, and calm settles over me. His deft fingers trail through my hair, skating over the silken strands in a soothing rhythm that lulls me into relaxation.

I'm somewhere between sleeping and waking.

Being with him like this feels like the sweetest dream, and I distantly marvel that this is real: my dark god is holding me like I'm his precious possession.

You were meant to be mine. His fierce declaration rumbles through my thoughts, and my gut tightens.

You love me. His remembered words hold the ring of command.

As though I don't have a choice in loving him.

My stomach knots, and my muscles tense.

He shushes me gently and continues stroking my hair in that hypnotic rhythm. I squeeze my eyes shut, longing to stay in the peaceful space with the man I love.

I'll keep you safe, Abigail. I will do anything to protect you.

A sharp image coalesces in my mind: Dane, covered in mud and a crimson spray that I don't want to contemplate.

He'd promised to protect me while his heart-breaking face had been splattered with blood.

And then...

A strong hand clamps over my mouth, muffling my scream for help. Dane's arm catches my vulnerable throat with familiar pressure, restricting my blood flow to my brain. I'm floating, but it's not a peaceful surrender. He's smothering me, subduing me.

The horrific memory layers over another dark night, the one that shattered my soul...

A gloved hand covers my nose and mouth, smothering my ability to draw breath. The shadows of my apartment close in, drawing me down into darkness. A low curse rumbles at my ear, and I'm suddenly released from the cruel grip. Oxygen floods my system, and my knees buckle. Strong arms catch me before I fall.

Dane's arms.

He's the masked man who violated me. He's GentAnon, my online confidante.

In all of those late-night correspondences with my anonymous, kinky kindred spirit, I revealed my most illicit, fucked-up fantasies.

And he made them come true.

You liked it. You came all over my hand.

The awful truth rakes at my heart with sharp black claws, and I choke on a painful gasp.

My first instinct is to jolt away from Dane, but I can already feel his bulky muscles coiling around me like a snake, ready to trap me in his perverse embrace.

I force myself to draw in a deep breath and keep my eyes closed. Disassociation comes easily. My mind goes mercifully blank, and my breaths come more naturally as I sink into nothingness. My body shuts down as though I was designed for this, and I'm too far gone to feel disgust over it. It's always been an act of self-preservation, a way to survive the horror of violation.

But I don't intend to surrender this time.

I allow the habitual disassociation to relax my body and shield my mind from the terror that hovers just at the edges of my thoughts. In response, Dane's powerful body relaxes around mine. He's satisfied with my submission, and he doesn't expect me to try to evade him.

I have to figure out where I am. I have dim, disjointed memories of a flight and an airport. He was holding my passport, back in that awful shrine to me in the powder blue house.

I'm not in Charleston.

Before I blacked out, he mentioned a journey *home*.

My stomach churns at the suspicion that he's taken me out of the country, but I breathe through it and resolutely remain detached from my tumultuous emotions.

"Where are we?" My voice is soft and oddly flat.

Dane caresses my cheek, but I keep my eyes

closed. I can't risk losing my tenuous, twisted form of serenity until I know more about my situation.

"We're in my family home in Yorkshire," he replies. "You'll be safe here."

Safe from who? The irate question flits at the periphery of my quiet bubble, and I choose to sink deeper into numbness.

"Don't worry, little dove. I'll take care of you."

Bile burns the back of my throat at the endearment; it's GentAnon's endearment for me.

The terrible reminder of what Dane really is shakes me to my core, and I suppress a shudder of pure revulsion.

"My friends will wonder where I am," I say, still soft and detached. "I can't be here."

He strokes my hair as though I'm an animal that could spook at the first sign of danger; as though I'm his pet, and he's keeping me calm.

"I used your phone to text Franklin. He knows you're on an extended vacation with me. And you don't need to worry about your barista job anymore. You can spend all of your time painting now."

My lungs seize for a moment, and I force in another breath.

"Stacy will expect me at the café," I try to reason.

"She's already accepted your notice." He says it

like a reassurance, not a trap. "She's been worried about you, and she didn't even try to demand that you come in for your final two weeks. You're free, Abigail."

His declaration would be laughable if my situation weren't so horrific. I'm caged in Dane's corded arms, and he's whisked me off to another country. I'm an ocean away from my friends, and my family won't bother to ask after me. He's easily extricated me from my life in Charleston with a few messages from my phone.

Finally, I open my eyes to fully assess where he's trapped me. I know now that I'm isolated from anyone who might care to check on me.

He's behind me, one arm pillowing my head while the other is loosely draped over my waist. He could tighten those powerful arms in an instant, so it's imperative that I remain calm.

I blink and look at my surroundings. I'm in an opulent bedroom, and I instinctively know that this house is from another era. Everything is impeccably arranged. The furnishings are obviously antiques, and the cream wallpaper is decorated with vines and delicate birds—a style that's clearly not contemporary.

Dane said this is his family home, and I

remember that he told me he comes from nobility. This house is likely grand, which means I'll probably struggle to find my way out quickly.

But if I can make it far enough away from him to scream for help, surely someone will hear. Someone will find me and take me away from the monster who's holding me so tenderly.

I'm lying on a massive four-poster bed with intricate carvings on the dark mahogany. There's a matching nightstand just in my line of vision, and a heavy brass lamp with a stained-glass shade sits atop it.

The door to the room is farther away, at least ten long strides across the patterned blue and gold rug.

I have to get out. I don't know the layout of this house, and I don't know how far away I am from someone who might help me.

But I have to get away from Dane before he drugs me again. Or before he violates me like he did when he was the masked man.

For so many years, I've frozen when threatened.

Now, my freedom depends on fighting back.

I surface from my disassociated state like I've broken through a heavy wave, and the world comes into sharp focus. My hand shoots out, and my fingers close around the brass lamp. I twist in Dane's hold just as his arms begin to tense around me. I can't afford to hesitate, not even when his gorgeous eyes flare with something like betrayal.

The stained-glass lampshade smashes against the side of his head, and his grip around me loosens.

I scramble free and leap off the bed, racing for the door.

I'm in the hallway when he bellows my name like an enraged beast.

My stomach drops. I didn't hit him hard enough. He's coming after me.

His lumbering steps stomp behind me, uneven at first, then quickening to match mine.

"Abigail!"

Regal portraits flicker by me on either side like I'm running through an aged film reel. There's a grand staircase at the end of the hall, and the light is brighter there. I dash toward it, breath sawing in and out of my lungs as I push myself impossibly faster.

But his strides are so much longer than mine, and he's pounding closer with every agonizingly long second. The hallway seems to lengthen, the light growing more distant. A primal scream rips from my chest as I propel myself forward, desperation clawing at my insides.

Someone has to hear. Someone has to help me.

Because I'm out of time.

The first step of the staircase drops beneath me, but before my foot makes contact with the aged wood, the iron band of his arm loops around my waist. He drags me back into his hard chest, and I shriek in terror and defiance.

"Let me go!"

The world tilts, and my belly collides with his shoulder. He lifts me up as though I weigh nothing, and his arm clamps down on my thighs. My legs jerk uselessly in his cruel hold. I can't get the leverage I need to kick out at him.

I slam my fists into his back and scream out my impotent rage.

I hear the sharp crack of his hand before the answering pain flares on my bottom.

"Calm down," he growls.

He *spanked* me. As though I'm a child having a tantrum.

I fight harder, punching his lower back with all my strength. A feral, warning sound rumbles from his chest, but I can't stop trying to get free.

"There's no use screaming," he says, unnervingly matter of fact. "No one will hear you."

"Because you're going to drug me again?" I bite back, writhing in his grip.

"No. Because I sent the staff away, and my family summers in Spain. We're the only two people for miles. Now, calm down."

A shrill laugh fills the bedroom, and I barely realize I'm making the maddened sound. "*Calm down?* You kidnapped me, Dane. You drugged me and brought me to another country. Let me go!"

He obliges me, and my stomach dips as I drop.

The soft mattress cushions my fall, and I immediately try to scramble away from him.

The monster is on me before I move an inch. His long fingers encircle my wrists, shackling them above my head. His other hand curves around my neck, threatening to squeeze if I continue to defy him. The weight of his body pins mine, and I squirm uselessly in his restraining hold.

"I can't let you go, Abigail." It's a calm statement of fact.

His perfect features might as well be carved from ice: frigid and unfeeling. If it weren't for the way his emerald eyes blaze, I'd think he was completely devoid of human emotion.

Blood trickles down his cheek from a small cut at his brow. I managed to inflict some damage when I struck him with the lamp, but it wasn't enough to save me.

"I won't go to the cops," I promise desperately. "I won't tell anyone what you did to me. Just let me go home."

His jaw ticks, and his eyes flare with a dark possessiveness that I recognize all too well.

"I can't let you go," he repeats, and it holds the solemn ring of a life sentence.

He's insane. The man I thought I loved is absolutely insane.

"Get your hands off me, psycho!"

He flinches, but his fingers firm around my neck, choking off my ability to hurl insults at him.

"I never claimed to be sane. I've let you see exactly what I am, and you begged for more."

My lips part on shallow breaths that barely squeeze through my constricted windpipe.

"Please…" I barely manage to whisper the plea.

"You like this, Abigail." The words are a dagger to my thrumming heart. "You want me. The real me."

"I don't know the real you," I gasp.

I don't want this monster who's holding me captive. He's not the fiercely protective man I fell for.

"Liar," he accuses coolly.

He releases my throat, and oxygen floods my system.

Horror hollows out my chest when his touch

trails lower. One strong hand keeps my wrists above my head, and the other deftly palms my breasts in the way I like best—just hard enough to threaten bruising pain.

My nipples peak against the inside of my bra, and a sickening pulse starts up between my legs.

"No," I moan in pure revulsion.

He knows my body. I told him my darkest secrets. He lured me into trusting him, and now he confidently manipulates pleasure from my deepest shame.

He's going to wield it against me like a weapon. It's far more devastating than the helplessness inflicted by the drugs.

"You do want me." It's a command, an edict. "You want it to be this way between us."

A drop of his blood drips from his tight jaw and sears my cheek. It mingles with my hot tears, and despair swallows me whole.

4

DANE

Three months ago

After I stalked Abigail home from the bar last night, I couldn't sleep. So, I return to her apartment building before six AM. Which is a good thing, because she leaves her building at six-thirty.

Judging by her black t-shirt and dark wash jeans, she's not going for a morning run. So, she's probably heading to work. Likely in the service industry, considering her simple outfit and the early hour.

I'm not usually one to ponder career choices, but I find myself wondering if she's content in her shabby little apartment with her low-paying job. A woman like Abigail should be dressed in silks and jewels, not practical cotton and jeans.

Once she's mine, I'll make sure to dress her up in a way that pleases me.

I shake off the strange thought and follow her down the street, keeping a careful distance so that she won't notice me.

I've never kept a woman before. It's never even crossed my mind. Not only do I get bored easily, but I know better than to risk forming a long-term relationship that might reveal my true nature over time.

A few nights with Abigail will surely be enough to sate my curiosity. And my lust.

My sleepless night wasn't only due to anticipation over seeing her again; I've wrestled with a raging hard-on ever since she trembled against me in the shadowy corner of the bar.

In another strange choice, I didn't slake my needs. Jerking off would have felt oddly like surrender. Defeat.

I will conquer Abigail, not the other way around. I won't allow anyone to make me feel weak. Certainly not a fragile, submissive woman.

I'm thoroughly in control of this seduction. She'll learn that soon enough.

We've only walked three blocks when she ducks into a small café. The lights are on, but the sign is still flipped to "closed". I check my watch. It's likely that the Sunny Side Café opens at seven. Possibly even later.

I harden my resolve. I'm not so desperate that I'll barge in the moment they open.

Abigail will need *me*, not the other way around. She'll beg and moan my name, and then I'll finally be satisfied.

She's disappeared into the back, so I can't even see her through the large windows that provide a clear view into the café.

I roll the odd tension from my shoulders and saunter off down the street.

I'll have to meet Meadows at our new premises by nine. Our practice officially starts operating next week, and we need to make sure everything is in order. We already have an impressive waitlist of patients, thanks to my partner's local connections and the shared reputation that we built in Baltimore.

Now that I'll have my own practice, I can be more discerning with my cases. And with my schedule.

I can make time for Abigail if I want to.

I smooth away my grimace at the errant thought.

The woman is getting under my skin, and I've barely spent an hour with her.

Surely, a little more time in her company is all I need to prove to myself that she's nothing special. Beautiful and beguiling, but not special.

She'll be imperfectly human, just like every other person I've ever met: simple and easily manipulated. Easily exercising control over everyone around me does satisfy me, but the shallow interactions can be tedious at times.

I wander away from the café for a while before I stop in one of the only open shops, where I buy an insipid magazine about local interests. Then I find a park bench where I can sit to pass the time for an hour or so.

While I wait to approach my prey, I can at least learn a little more about my new home here in Charleston. My patients are gratified when I show interest in their small little lives. It's irksome, but it'll help grow the practice. I'll earn even more money, be even more secure.

I don't need my family's fortune to live a life of luxury. The first few years of university were hard, but nothing will ever make me go begging for a handout from my father.

You'll be back. My mother's final, spiteful words

echo through my mind. *You can't make it on your own, Daniel. You can't embarrass the family like this. What will our friends say if you give up your title and run away to America like a pathetic coward who can't face his duties?*

I shake off the memory and redirect my focus to the article about an upcoming garden tour in Charleston's historic districts.

I haven't thought about that altercation with my mother in years.

It's possible that Abigail's obvious financial struggles are making me recall the years when I had to scrape by, too, before I earned my medical degree and established my reputation as a skilled surgeon.

I manage to read another article about a nearby plantation before I think about the wad of one dollar bills Abigail pulled out of her wallet when she tried to pay for her cocktail last night.

I used to be frugal with my money, too, when I had nothing more than a small stipend from my scholarship at Johns Hopkins.

Now, I'm more than wealthy enough to buy an expensive home in Harleston Village. I'll never be poor again.

And as long as I choose to keep Abigail with me, she will want for nothing. I won't be seen neglecting a woman who's on my arm. I can provide for her, and I won't allow anyone to think otherwise.

Clean up, Daniel. What will our friends think if they see you with bloody knuckles?

I hear my mother's voice again. Always so concerned with appearances, not with why her ten-year-old son might have blood on his hands.

I crumple the magazine in my fists.

I loathe pretentious people who perform for the sake of others, but I can't deny that I've been forced to live my life with my civilized mask firmly in place. I learned at a young age that I can't get what I want if I let people see the monster inside; charm works much better than fear.

I gnash my teeth and toss the magazine in a public rubbish bin. These irritating thoughts aren't something I often contemplate, and I don't know why they're troubling me now.

Must be the sleepless night messing with my usual composure.

I run a hand over my hair to smooth it into a neater style and stride toward the café. It's just past eight AM now. Surely, they'll be open.

The glass door isn't locked, so I'm able to stride into the Sunny Side Café with smooth confidence.

Abigail is almost entirely hidden behind the

espresso machine that dominates the end of the counter; only the top of her brunette head and the barest hint of delicately arched brows are visible.

Is she shy even in her workplace? Last night, I surmised that she's a bit anxious in social situations. I'd enjoyed riding that edge, making her nervous while drawing out her forbidden lust.

"Good morning! How are you?"

I blink and redirect my attention to the pretty woman behind the register. Her name badge says *Stacy*. She must be Abigail's friend, the one they couldn't find at the bar last night when Franklin so rudely dragged my prey away from me.

My drunken prey.

I smother a frown as I remember Abigail's slurred speech and the way she'd leaned on her male friend for support.

Even if he hadn't taken her out of the bar to look for Stacy, I wouldn't have been able to satisfy my lust last night. Not when Abigail was intoxicated.

It would've been much easier to track her down if we'd exchanged numbers, though. Less risky than following her.

I arrange my features into my usual charming smile and sharpen my focus. My prey is within my sights once again. She won't escape this time.

"I'm well, thank you," I say in response to Stacy's inane question. This Carolina pretense at politeness will take some getting used to.

Although, looking into Stacy's large brown eyes, she does seem more interested in me than rote niceties. I'm used to attention from women, but there's only one that I want to captivate now.

"What can I get for you?" Stacy's voice drops slightly deeper, an invitation rather than simply taking my order.

I keep my smile in place but don't allow it to tilt in anticipation of a flirtation. Usually, I'd enjoy toying with this woman. In a slew of social interactions that are so often mundane, making people flustered so that they'll trip over themselves to please me is mildly amusing.

"I'll have an Americano, please." My tone is warm and friendly, but nothing more.

Abigail probably wouldn't like it if I were rude to Stacy; they're friends, after all.

"What's your name?"

I pause for a moment and quirk a brow at Stacy. She's being quite forward, and I'm here for Abigail.

"For your cup," she explains when I don't answer right away.

I don't fully buy it, but I suppose it's probably

common practice at their café to write names on cups to keep track of orders.

"Dane," I introduce myself.

I can't stop my gaze from cutting toward the espresso machine, but Abigail doesn't appear when I say my name.

"You don't sound like you're from around here," Stacy observes, leaning toward me slightly.

"I'm not." I suppress a sigh. My English accent often elicits this comment, and I'm getting impatient to speak to Abigail.

The sound of my voice doesn't seem to have attracted her attention. She liked my accent when we spoke last night. Why isn't she turning to greet me?

I anticipate her slight surprise at this "chance" second meeting: the way those pretty rosebud lips will part on a little intake of breath, and her remarkable aquamarine eyes will widen.

Maybe she's shyer than I thought. And she's sober now, so that might make her even more reticent to approach me. Is she embarrassed at how inebriated she was?

Curiosity consumes me. I forget to continue my polite conversation with Stacy and prowl down the length of the bar.

Abigail appears in profile. Her lips are slightly pursed as she focuses so intently on pouring out latte art that she doesn't seem aware of my presence. Those lovely eyes are fixed on the steamed milk, but even from a side view, the light catches in the aqua pools, illuminating them like the Mediterranean Sea on a sunny day.

"Good morning," I greet, prompting her attention.

"Morning." She barely breathes the word, but her mouth quirks in a pleasant smile.

The perfectly polite, good Carolina girl is back.

But I know her secret now.

I'm not good. She whispered her forbidden truths last night when she tormented me with her responses to my dark questions.

She wears a mask, just like I do. Her genteel veneer hides a sensual woman with taboo desires: an inner darkness that complements my own.

Unlike me, she's not cold and calculated. She's guileless and soft.

The perfect match for my cruel needs.

But she's still not looking at me. She's finished her latte art, but she's moved on to grinding the espresso for my Americano.

She must be embarrassed about last night. I'll

put her at ease by speaking in my practiced bedside manner tone. I won't allow any shame to get in the way of our connection.

"How are you feeling today?" I ask, noting the faint dark circles under her eyes.

I wonder if she has a headache from drinking too much. If so, I'll make sure she takes a break to drink water and eat something before taking ibuprofen. I'm sure I can charm Stacy into allowing her colleague a moment to collect herself.

Abigail's careful smile remains fixed in place, and she places a paper cup with my name on it beneath the espresso machine.

Irritation makes my own charming smile waver. I'm not sure how much longer I can tolerate this reticence.

"I'm fine, thanks," she replies softly. "How are you?"

The rote question doesn't hold the same depth of true interest that Stacy showed me. It's a bland social nicety, a requirement for her job.

I'm finding her shyness annoying this morning rather than intriguing. Maybe pursuing her was a mistake. If she can't bring herself to make eye contact unless her inhibitions are lowered by alcohol, she might be too tedious to hold my attention.

"I'm feeling good," I reply with forced nonchalance.

This is definitely getting tedious. I don't want to engage in small talk with her.

"The whiskey at the dive bar last night wasn't good enough to tempt me to drink more than two."

"Oh," she says blandly. "I don't know much about whiskey unless it's mixed with Coke."

My smile quirks despite my irritation, and I indulge in one of her secrets. "You prefer sweeter drinks."

She blinks, and we finally make eye contact. Her pale cheeks flush a perfect shade of pink, and I think she's about to thank me for the cosmopolitans I bought her last night. Instead, her gaze is a bit wary.

"Yeah, I guess I'm a cliché. I do enjoy girly, pink drinks."

I don't understand her strange energy. Her eyes are keen on mine, but they're guarded.

"Do you want milk in your Americano, Dane?"

She says my name, but it's not husky with remembered lust. There's no familiarity in the way she addresses me.

It takes me a full three seconds to realize that she doesn't recognize me. Apparently, she was so drunk last night that she blacked out our meeting.

I'm silent for too long, because she fills the awkward moment with a nervous laugh.

"I guess not. Black Americano, got it."

She puts a lid on the cup that has my name written on it and places it on the counter between us.

Something tightens my gut, a strange sensation that I've felt before, but never to this degree. The pang is harsh enough to make me grimace.

Anger.

I'm angry that she doesn't remember me. She doesn't remember *us*, the electric connection we share.

She drops her lovely eyes and quickly returns to her espresso machine. Her fingers tremble slightly as she reaches for the milk jug.

I realize that I'm scowling.

I never lose control of my facial expression.

"I'm sorry," I say as smoothly as I can manage. The last thing I want is to scare her off.

I'm more than just annoyed, but I'm finding the intensity of my response to her fascinating, even if it is unpleasant.

"I was short with you. I suppose I might've had more whiskey last night than I thought. A bit of a headache this morning." The lie comes easily. "The coffee will help. Thank you."

"No worries. Enjoy!" Her sunny smile is back, but she keeps her focus on her work.

Fuck.

I intimidated her.

How did this go so badly? I'd expected to saunter into the café and sweep her off her feet. We should be exchanging numbers right now, and she's supposed to be sitting across from me at a sumptuous dinner in a few hours.

And she's meant to be screaming my name in my bed shortly thereafter.

Instead, she won't even look at me.

An odd feeling comes over me again, and I'm more reluctant to acknowledge this one.

Insecurity?

The ground feels like it's shifting under my feet, and the angry churning in my gut has been replaced by a disconcerting knotting sensation.

It's unpleasant and completely foreign to me.

Fascinating.

Suddenly, I'm eager to know what other new feelings this puzzle of a woman might elicit from me. I'm currently experiencing a spectrum of discomfiting emotions. But there's the other side of the coin, too.

What would it be like to experience more than cruel, fleeting pleasure?

What ecstatic high will I achieve when she murmurs my name like a prayer and begs me for an orgasm only I can give her?

"I'm new to the area," I say instead of leaving her side. "I'm sure I'll see you again."

Her nervous laugh fills the space between us. "We do have good coffee here," she allows. "And we always love getting new regulars."

"I'll see you tomorrow morning, then." It's a promise, and it comes out in a rougher, more intense tone than I intended.

A light shiver races over her fragile frame.

Arousal at the hint of danger? Or fear at my masculine attention?

Maybe both.

The impulse to grasp that alluring purple curl and tug her toward me makes my fingers furl at my side.

I force myself to relax. That would be far too frightening, and I'd probably end up in the back of a cop car.

I'm clinging to my control by my fingernails. It's horrifying and fascinating in equal measure.

I have to leave before I say something else that I'll regret. Abigail will be here whenever I want to see her. I'll find a way to lure her into my bed.

"Have a great day!" she says in that falsely bright tone.

It's so practiced that I almost believe it.

I summon up my own familiar mask and offer her one final charming smile before I stroll out of the café. I barely suppress a grimace at the bitterness of the espresso on my tongue. Usually, I take my coffee with a splash of milk and one sugar, but Abigail thinks I like it black now. I can endure the bitterness to avoid further awkwardness.

I'll come back for her.

I recall her submissive responses to my firm commands last night. She must be pliable enough for me to seduce her without too much difficulty.

Then I can explore and master these strange new *feelings.*

I'll fuck her out of my system, and then everything will go back to normal.

5

ABIGAIL

Now

Dane's sensual lips twist in a frown, and a furrow creases his brow. He keeps my wrists shackled in one hand, and his weight still pins me.

I drag in a shuddering breath when he releases my breasts to brush away the wetness that sears my cheeks. He lifts his fingers to inspect them, and his frown deepens. His crimson blood is diluted by my tears, and the two mingle into a glistening red stream that rolls down his palm.

He looks...puzzled. Like he can't fathom why I'm so distressed.

Or maybe he can't believe that I actually fought back and made him bleed.

I lift my chin and glare up at him with open defiance.

"If you violate me, I will hate you," I hiss. "My body will respond, but I will hate you."

His eyes glitter when they fix on mine again. He's peering at me like I'm some alien creature he doesn't understand.

"But you like when I make you cry."

I gape at him even as my stomach turns at the truth in his words.

"Not like this." I force the denial through my constricted throat. "And never again. I trusted you. I thought I knew you."

His eyes flash. "You do know me. I've let you see me in a way I've never shown myself to anyone. You chose me. You love me."

"Stop saying that!" My words are roughened by desperation. I think I'll vomit if he says it again. "How can I love a stranger? How can I love the masked man who assaulted me?"

He shakes his head, as though my words irritate him like swarming gnats.

"You weren't supposed to find out about that."

"You think that's the problem here? That I found out, not that you attacked me in my home?" I glower at him, allowing him to see the depth of my disgust. "I know what you really are now. I could never love you after what you did to me."

He blinks, and his expression smooths to stony, unfeeling planes once again. "You're upset. I understand that you didn't agree to leave Charleston. But things will be better for you now. You don't have to scrape by with your barista job anymore. You don't have to live in that shitty old apartment. I'll provide a life for you that you deserve, Abigail."

My jaw goes slack for a moment. The depth of his delusion is truly unfathomable.

"I want the life I built for myself." I defy him. "I don't want anything from you. I want to go home and never see you again."

His eyes narrow. "That's not happening. You're mine. Nothing will change that."

"Saying I'm yours doesn't make it true," I shoot back. "I won't willingly give myself to you."

"You signed the contract," he reminds me.

"I signed a contract with the man I met at the café. I signed myself over to the Dane that I knew.

The Dane who promised to protect me and honor my consent. You are not that man."

A shadow flutters at his jaw. "You didn't meet me at the café. You don't even remember the night we met because you drank too much and blacked it out. Do you know how maddening it was to see you all those mornings, and you looked at me like I was just another customer? Like we hadn't shared something unique?"

"What are you talking about?" I demand.

"We met at the bar a few nights after I moved to Charleston. You told me your dark desires, and I let you see a glimpse of the real me. You wanted me then, and I only let you go when I realized you were too drunk. I didn't want you to regret being with me.

"So, I found out where you worked. I approached you the next morning, and you had no idea who I was. What we had shared. What we could have been so much sooner if you hadn't been so stubbornly evasive."

My mouth opens and then closes. I'm not sure what to say in response to this new revelation. It's not completely unbelievable that I might've had too much to drink on a night out; I like a cocktail or three to ease my inhibitions when I go dancing.

I think back to that first morning I met him—the first time I remember meeting him.

He'd acted so strange at the café. Intense and familiar in a way that unnerved me.

But then, I convinced myself that I'd just been nervous because he's so gorgeous. I could barely look at him when he came in for his daily Americano because he's intimidatingly handsome.

Now I know that he made me nervous because deep down, part of me knew he was a predator. I have no idea what happened between us at the bar, but it must've been dark enough to set my senses on high alert in his presence. That giddy, fizzy hit of adrenaline had made me enamored with him on our first date.

I didn't recognize the thrill for what it was: a primal warning of danger.

My mind catches on something odd that he just said. "And how did you know where I worked?"

His gaze cuts away from mine for a heartbeat, and then his eyes narrow with something like defiance.

"I followed you home when you left the bar. You stumbled off before we could truly get to know each other. How else was I supposed to find you again?"

He makes stalking me sound so reasonable.

"You could have simply asked for my number, like a normal man."

His beautiful face hardens to a grim mask. "I am not a normal man. I thought you knew that. I thought you accepted me, just like I accept everything that you are. You're perfect for me, Abigail. Why are you denying us now?"

I shake my head. He's clearly insane, completely deluded. He seems incapable of understanding how stalking and assaulting me was a violation on the deepest level.

"There is no *us*." I try to speak as calmly as possible when my heart is hammering against my ribcage. "You're not the man I thought you were. Your belief that I love you won't change that."

He bares his teeth at me like a cornered predator, and for a moment, I think he's going to hurt me.

I cringe, and suddenly, his weight is gone.

He's standing three feet away from where I lie sprawled on the bed, completely disoriented by his abrupt decision to release me.

"You'll want to get freshened up before I show you around the estate," he says, the perfectly composed, genteel host. He tips his head in the direction of an ensuite bathroom. "Go on. I'll wait here for you."

Now that he's mentioned it, I become acutely aware of the fact that I've neglected my basic needs. How long was I unconscious?

My cheeks heat, and I duck past him into the bathroom.

Once I'm a bit more composed, I splash cold water onto my flushed face. The awful weight of my new reality presses down on my shoulders like a ton of lead, and it's all I can do to keep my shaking knees from buckling. I grip the sink for support. My knuckles are almost as white as the porcelain.

I'm alone with a madman on a remote estate. He's already proven that he's so much stronger than I am. Fighting him only gave him an excuse to pin me down and attempt to coax shameful pleasure from my unwilling body.

I won't make that mistake again.

Dane doesn't value my consent. That much has become painfully clear.

He thinks I love him. If I can convince him that I will never feel a shred of affection for him again, he might let me go. He seems obsessed with his misguided belief that I belong to him. Once he accepts that I will never surrender my heart, he'll grow tired of me. He'll release me, and I can return home to Charleston.

I straighten my spine and face myself in the mirror. I take several deep breaths and convince myself that my plan will work.

It has to work.

Because the ache in the center of my chest is from more than just the fearful pounding of my heart. I did love Dane, and the loss has shattered something inside me. Being near the monster who wears his face will be agonizing, but I'll have to bear it.

My freedom depends on it.

His soft knock on the door draws a shocked yelp from my tight chest.

"Let me in, Abigail."

"I'm coming out."

I don't want him to break down the door to get to me.

I slide the lock back, and he towers over me. I swallow hard and edge away from him. He follows my movement, staying resolutely in my personal space.

"What are you doing?" I demand breathlessly.

He gingerly touches two fingers to the bloody cut on his brow. "I need to get cleaned up. Stay."

He issues the command like I'm a wayward pet. I

grit my teeth against the tirade that teases at the tip of my tongue.

I will remain compliant. I won't give him the excuse to manhandle me again.

My wits will get me out of this. I have to keep them sharp, and I know his unwelcome touch will devastate me.

He hisses softly when he cleans the cut I inflicted, but he doesn't rebuke me for attacking him. I'm relieved he doesn't lash out in reprisal for the pain I caused him.

My heart breaks all over again. The Dane I loved would've done anything to protect me. He cherished me, and I trusted that he would never harm me.

This monster who kidnapped me is completely unpredictable. He was capable of holding a knife to my throat while he violated me. He could turn violent at any moment, so I have to remain calm and not give him any reason to harm at me.

He doesn't look at me for the few minutes it takes him to find a pack of bandages in the medicine cabinet. It's almost as though he's ignoring me—if it weren't for the menace rolling off him in waves. His every movement is tense with barely leashed aggression, but, mercifully, he doesn't try to assault me again.

When he turns to face me, the blood has been washed from his face, and the only sign of the wound I gave him is a tiny bandage on his forehead. His midnight hair tumbles over his brow, almost concealing it entirely.

He sweeps the unruly locks back, smoothing them into his usual neat style. He's completely unruffled and utterly composed when he holds out his hand like a gentleman.

I stare at it, unwilling to place my hand within his grasp. My fists clench at my sides in silent defiance. His sharp gaze flicks over my rigid posture, and he shrugs.

He drops his hand to his side as though the tense exchange doesn't bother him in the slightest, but his jaw remains tight enough that a shadow flits at his cheek.

"I'll show you around the house," he says in a smooth cadence.

I get the bizarre sense that he thinks I'm his honored guest, not his captive.

The man truly is insane. How did I not see it before?

I recall the times his face went cold, and his eyes glinted with green fire. I'd trembled with fear-drenched desire, but that was when I trusted him implicitly. Before I found out that he's the masked man. Before I knew that he hid behind GentAnon's screenname to learn all of my most forbidden desires.

He claims that we met the night before he first came into the café. The fact that he stalked me on my way home and then followed me to work the next morning makes a chill pebble my skin.

All those months, he came into the café like clockwork every morning.

Until the day he finally asked me on a date.

The day after the masked man—*Dane,* I silently correct myself—attacked me.

"Why?" The single word is a razor blade in my throat, dragging its way out of me.

I don't think I want to know, but I can't help asking. I can still barely accept what's happening to me, and I'm desperate to understand.

"Why did you ask me out? Why do any of this?"

His green eyes blaze, burning into me. "Because you're perfect for me."

6

DANE

Three Months Ago

I've visited the café every morning for a week, and Abigail is simply polite to me, as though I'm like every other customer.

It's frustrating.

Infuriating.

So, I find myself strolling through her neighborhood after the sun sets. She won't even look at me when I'm at the café. I must've thoroughly intimidated her when I completely misjudged the situation. I'd been overly familiar after our meeting at the bar, and she hadn't remembered me at all.

I can't harass her while she's at work; that'll only raise more red flags.

But now that I'm a regular at the café, I can't approach her elsewhere without seeming like I'm stalking her. I'd only spook her even more.

I force my clenched jaw to loosen.

This woman is maddening, but the more difficult it is to pursue her, the more I crave to conquer her.

I've never been evaded by a woman before. No one has wanted to evade me.

But Abigail is a stubborn exception in so many ways.

I will learn her secrets, and then she will submit to me. Once she surrenders, I'll be able to move on from this dangerous fixation.

I shouldn't be here. It's risky to follow her home.

And I never put myself at risk. I refuse to do anything foolish that might end with me behind bars. I'll never be caged.

I'm too smart for that.

I glance around the deserted street. This isn't the nicest neighborhood, but it's quiet.

Probably because no one seems to want to live in the dilapidated houses that surround her ramshackle apartment building. There's small, narrow house directly across the street. The powder blue paint on the exterior is peeling, and it's dark inside. No one's home.

The garden is overgrown, and that suits my desires. I duck beneath unruly foliage and push open the rusty gate. Within less than a minute, I settle into the shadows provided by the azalea and hydrangea bushes that haven't been pruned in years.

Abigail's window is a yellow rectangle shining through the night. At this distance, I can see her slim form moving around her cramped living room. She's setting up an easel.

Curiosity nips at me, an insistent bite.

So, my pretty prey is an artist. I'm not surprised to learn that she has a creative streak. Her quirky purple curl and the whimsical badges I've noted on her work apron indicate a playful energy that defies stricter social norms for a woman of her age. Her unicorn pin surprised me when I noted it on my second visit to the café, but I've since decided that I find it charming. The smiling iced coffee and frowning broccoli are a bit odder, but her quirkiness makes more sense now that I see her with a paintbrush in her delicate hand.

Despite her perfectly polite demeanor and sunny smiles, Abigail isn't a conformist. She marches to the beat of her own drum. Maybe that's why I'm having such a difficult time pinning her down.

If I can just learn what makes her tick, she'll be in my bed, and this strange new fixation will finally be satisfied.

Her hand moves in small, elegant strokes as she works with fluidity but precision. I can only see the back of her brunette head from this angle, but I have a clear view of her canvas.

She's too far away for me to make out the details of her painting. For a while, I'm content to simply watch her graceful, minute movements as she works. But the longer she continues, the more I crave to know what absorbs her attention so completely.

I retrieve my phone from my pocket and open the camera in an attempt to zoom in on her art. But the lighting is too imbalanced at this distance for me to make out more than a navy-blue blur on her canvas.

I frown and tuck my phone back in my pocket.

If I could learn more about her art, I might be able to capture her attention when we make small talk at the café.

I resolve that I have to know the subject of her painting. I'll learn Abigail's secrets, and she will submit to me.

No one seems to live in the powder blue house across the street from Abigail's apartment. I took some time to peer into the darkened windows before settling into the shadows of the overgrown garden. The house is devoid of furnishings, and the peeling wallpaper inside is in even worse condition than the exterior paint.

It's a convenient arrangement for me; I can watch my prey without concern about being interrupted.

After my frustration last night, I came prepared. I lean back in the rickety garden chair and lift the binoculars I purchased this afternoon.

The back of Abigail's head appears in sharp relief, brunette waves shining in the golden light cast by her cheap standing lamps. Her voluminous hair is tamed into a loose braid, and the pretty amethyst streak weaves through the darker locks. I want to wrap that braid around my fist and use it to anchor her to me while I plunder her lush mouth.

Her canvas is still propped up on the easel in the middle of her living room, but she's sitting on her couch now. Some maddened urge to keep my focus on her prevents me from shifting my attention to the painting for a full minute.

But she's on her laptop, probably browsing social media or something equally mundane. I'd much prefer to see her paint again, especially now that I'm equipped to view her art properly.

I blow out a sigh and focus on the unfinished painting instead. It's a stunning impressionist landscape, depicting a pristine beach before an incoming storm. The sand is captured in textured strokes of pale yellow, indicating a sunny day before the encroaching tempest. At the horizon, turbulent, dark navy waves surge, so at odds with the peaceful beach.

I wonder if this is a scene she's painting from memory, or if it's an embellishment.

I've never seen a storm like it.

But then again, I've never really paid much attention to the natural world. I prefer to spend my time amongst people rather than pondering my surroundings in solitude. I can control people, not the weather. So, nature doesn't interest me much. It's just a backdrop, scenery for the psychological games that keep me amused.

But there's something compelling about Abigail's art. I can't quite put my finger on why I'm still staring at the painting when I could be watching her instead.

I shake off the odd compulsion to continue studying the stormy sea and focus on her braided hair again. The shade of dark purple is truly lovely against her brunette locks. I admire the way it weaves through her thick waves, how the heavy braid is loose enough to conceal most of her nape. I get the smallest glimpse of bare skin where her neck meets her shoulder, which is covered by her soft black work shirt.

She hasn't bothered to change after finishing her shift; she's gone straight to her laptop.

Why isn't she painting?

I'm scowling in the darkness, and I smooth away the unbidden expression of displeasure.

I'm losing control around her, and even if no one is here to see it, my cheeks still flush with a strange heat.

I definitely don't like the sensation, so I choose to ignore this particular new *feeling* she's eliciting.

I'll have her under my control soon enough.

What is she so absorbed with at her laptop?

I try to focus the binoculars on her screen, but whatever she's viewing is too bright and small for me to make out more than a white blur. Her fingers fly over the keyboard.

She's typing something, and the deft, rapid

strokes of her delicate fingers fascinate me almost as much as the strokes of her paintbrush.

I'm not sure how long I indulge myself in watching her elegant hands before she puts her laptop away. When she stands up from where she was seated on the couch, she turns toward her bedroom rather than her canvas. I can see her in profile now, and her porcelain cheek is flushed a gorgeous shade of pink.

It reminds me of the alluring shade of her blush when we first met at the bar last week.

What was she writing that has her cheeks turning pink?

I'm burning for answers, but all I'm met with is darkness when she turns off the lights. She disappears into her bedroom. I can't see into it because this window only provides me a view into her living room.

I could prowl around her building to find out what she's doing now, but that would be even riskier than watching her from this shadowed garden. I'd be out in the open, and one of her neighbors might see me peering into her window.

I force my jaw to unclench and put the binoculars away. I'll come back tomorrow night. I have to know more.

SHE'S BACK at her easel, but the canvas is darker tonight. I had to stay at work later than I would've liked, so she's already deeply absorbed in her art by the time I finally settle into the rickety garden chair.

I'd anticipated watching her storm-tossed sea develop into a towering tempest, but she seems to have a different subject in mind tonight.

Heavy strokes of midnight black darken the edges of the canvas, and all of the light she captures with her paintbrush is focused on the center of her painting. Shadows cling to creamy flesh, as though they're drawing her subject deeper into their forbidden embrace. They curl around a slender neck like tendrils of smoke, and the distinctly feminine chin is tipped back as though to welcome the dark claim.

The knife at her subject's throat glints dully, a charcoal gray that's almost forged from the shadows that caress their victim.

Rosebud lips are parted on a gasp that's undeniably erotic. And just at the bottom edge of the painting, two peaked, pink nipples beg for attention.

My teeth clench hard enough to make my jaw

ache, and my cock stiffens to the point of discomfort in the confines of my jeans.

I was right to think that Abigail's desires are a perfect match for my own. She secretly fantasizes about being threatened and forced to experience transcendent pleasure.

I've never allowed myself to truly frighten a woman. There are certain parameters I have to operate within to fit social norms, even in more deviant subcultures. Those boundaries have irked me in the past, but now, they feel like the iron bars of a cage that's far too small to contain me.

What would it be like to throw off those invisible constraints and truly unleash myself upon her? Would she welcome the thrill of this darkest game?

I have no desire to harm my pretty prey; on the contrary, I'll do anything to shield her so that she'll welcome me back into her body again and again.

I know now that a few nights with this woman won't be enough.

The thought makes something slither down my spine.

Apprehension?

If I allow my mask to drop around Abigail, my secrets will be exposed. I'll put myself at risk.

If I push her too far, she might scream in horror

when I show her my true self. I could lose everything I've worked so hard for these last fifteen years: my wealth, my reputation, my freedom.

The temptation to indulge in this most forbidden connection is almost enough to drive me to madness, but I can't give in. I can't take on that risk.

Yet.

Until I know for sure that Abigail won't be repulsed by my crueler advances, I have to be patient. I can watch her. Study her.

And when it comes to my studies, I've always excelled. I have an eye for detail and an excellent memory.

Abigail will be my greatest conquest, and I'll devote the time and effort necessary to get what I want: her, in my bed, screaming my name.

I've never faced such a thrilling challenge in my life, and the prospect makes intense pleasure gather at the base of my spine. The temptation of her sensual painting is almost enough to make me come undone without the touch of her delicate hand.

I take a breath and master the bizarre urge to surrender to the insistent pleasure. I'm not going to come in my pants when Abigail is out of my reach.

She's not in control of this seduction. I am.

She just doesn't know it yet.

7

ABIGAIL

Now

You're perfect for me.

I press my lips together to hold back the defiant words that burn my tongue. Or maybe that's the bile that's creeping up my throat.

I swallow hard against my rising nausea and wrench my gaze from his burning green stare. The possessiveness in his eyes is terrifyingly potent, and I can't bear to maintain the intense connection for one second longer. He truly believes what he's saying. I'm not sure if it'll be possible to convince him that he's completely delusional.

He's decided that I belong to him.

When I look into his fiercely handsome face, I see the man I fell in love with. It's beyond horrific to know that man was never real. Everything moment we've shared has been a manipulation.

I hug my arms around my aching chest, as though I can hold the shattered pieces of my heart together.

"You must be hungry," he says, voice warm with concern.

I can't trust in that warmth. I've seen his cold, merciless soul now. Any display of tenderness must be just another lie to lure me in.

I've always known that Dane is wickedly intelligent. I just didn't realize that he was using that razor sharp mind against me. He's a convincing enough actor that he tricked me into falling in love with him.

If I hadn't gone into the powder blue house and found out what he really is, I would still be in love with him. I'd be in his bed back in Charleston, calling him *Master* and giving my body to him eagerly.

I shudder at the thought. Because part of me wishes I could be that version of me—ignorant to Dane's true nature. His crimes against me.

"I don't feel like eating anything," I say truthfully.

I'm not sure if I can keep food down when my gut is churning so violently.

"You haven't eaten in nearly twenty-four hours." His voice is heavy with admonishment now. "Come with me."

He reaches for me, and I recoil. His hand clenches to a fist, then withdraws.

"You'll feel better once you've had food." He says it like I'm being unreasonable and providing me with sustenance will make me less cranky. "You will eat, Abigail."

I bristle at the command, and I keep my eyes trained on the black and white tiles beneath my feet. After a tense moment, I manage to force my head to dip in a jerky nod.

Remaining in this bathroom won't get me closer to freedom. If we truly are alone and isolated on his estate, I need to explore my cage. I won't try to run again unless I'm certain that I have a chance of evading him. For now, I'll remain complaint. He can compel my actions, but he can't rule my heart.

The sooner he accepts the fact that I will never love him—that I feel nothing but revulsion for him—the sooner he'll tire of me and release me.

He doesn't reach for me again, and I huff out a small, relieved breath. I keep my eyes averted from his powerful body as I follow him through the bedroom. My gaze catches on the shattered remnants of the colorful, stained-glass lampshade that litter the rug, and for an insane moment, I consider snatching up one of the jagged shards to wield it as a weapon.

I grit my teeth and force my reluctant feet to carry me away from temptation. I can't afford to attack him and lose.

We make our way down the long corridor, heading toward the staircase I never quite reached during my mad escape attempt. I focus on the layout of my surroundings, noting three closed doors that interrupt the lines of portraits on either side of me.

Dane notices my swinging gaze and explains, "There are four bedrooms in this wing. My brother, James, and I have rooms here. My parents occupy the east wing, although there are a further six guest rooms that remain empty. Not including the additional accommodations in the carriage house."

My heart sinks at the sprawling description of the manor. I'll have to rely on Dane to navigate the space.

We descend the wide staircase and cross a cavernous foyer. Natural light pours through large windows on either side of what I assume is the front door, making the wood paneled walls glow like they're burnished.

Dane leads me through a maze of rooms, and I commit the grand spaces to memory. There's a robin's egg blue sitting room with intricate crown molding. A dining room with a table long enough to host a feast like something out of a period drama. A library with thousands of books lining every wall on intricately carved shelves.

"I'll show you the billiards room and the indoor pool later," he says, making genial conversation. "There's a fully equipped gym, too, but we can exercise outdoors if you prefer. The Yorkshire Dales are too beautiful to waste time on a treadmill."

We enter a massive kitchen with modern appliances that have been tastefully chosen to complement the historic character of the space. Dark wood beams accent the cream ceiling overhead, and the massive stone fireplace beside a large, oval dining table is swept clean for summer. Across from the marble-topped island, the kitchen opens up into a glass-walled conservatory.

My breath catches when I get my first look at the stunning countryside. Verdant, grassy hills roll to the horizon, and a narrow river is a shining blue ribbon that meanders between them. It spills into a huge lake that must be several miles away. I don't see any other houses—only dry-stone walls crisscrossing the hills, which are dotted with distant white sheep.

We truly are isolated in this gorgeous landscape.

My fingers itch for my paintbrush even as my stomach turns. The urge to capture the way the sunlight dapples the green hills is an ever-present, irrepressible artistic calling.

But the rural setting fills my heart with dread.

There's no one here to help me. No neighbors to hear me if I scream.

"I'll make us a proper fry-up," Dane says, calling my attention away from the terribly beautiful countryside. "It might take me a moment to get my bearings. Cooking in this kitchen is a novelty. All of my meals were prepared for me when I was a boy. In the years since I moved to America, I've learned to take care of myself."

His lopsided smile is so perfectly charming that I marvel at his ability to mask his monstrous nature.

"I can make a decent meal for you." He says it like a reassurance. "I doubt my brother could manage it. He's never worked at anything a day in his life."

"You brother still lives here? With your parents?" I try to keep my tone casual, politely interested.

He sees right through me. "Like I said, they're summering abroad. And no, my brother has his faults, but he has no desire to remain close to our parents. I believe he prefers to spend his time in the Wensleydale lodge. It's only about a half hour's drive from here, but it permits him some distance from our mother."

"You said you left your family behind when you moved to America for college," I say carefully. "Won't they want to see you now that you're back home?"

He scoffs. "If they knew I was here, they'd try to find a way to lock me down and prevent me from leaving. But don't worry. I paid the staff to keep quiet. They were happy to take an extended holiday."

"So, you're not planning to stay."

I have to get a sense of his plans for me. Does he intend to return to Charleston at some point? It certainly sounds as though he doesn't want to stay here for long.

He frowns and turns his attention to the fridge. He doesn't look at me when he replies, "You and I need to come to an understanding before we go back to the States. Meadows is pissed that I fucked off to England without notice, but he'll have to manage the practice without me for a while. I told him my grandmother had passed away. I just didn't specify when."

He keeps his focus on finding the pans he needs rather than looking at me.

"You think I'll turn you in for what you did to me," I surmise quietly.

In profile, I note the downward twist of his sensual lips, as though he's bitten into something sour.

"I don't intend to go to prison." His voice is smooth and cultured as ever, entirely unruffled except for his frown. "You need some time to process what you saw. I understand that. It's regrettable that I had to bring you here, but it was the best option."

"You think kidnapping me was the best option." It's a dull, flat statement. I have to keep the shrill accusation from my tone if I'm going to reason with him. He has to hear how insane this is when I put it in clear, plain language.

He places several fat sausages and four rashers of thick bacon onto a hot pan, and the meat instantly begins to sizzle. He continues to focus on cooking, his movements smooth and utterly casual, as though this is a normal morning and nothing is troubling him.

"You don't have to continue with your menial job

to make ends meet anymore," he reasons. "You can spend all your time focusing on your art. That's what you want, isn't it? I can give that to you, Abigail. I have given it to you. You're free to reach your full potential now."

"You stole my phone and quit my job for me." It takes all my willpower to remain calm and rational. "You made my friends believe that I'm willingly on vacation with you. But you drugged me, and you're holding me against my will. That's not freedom, Dane. That's captivity."

He shrugs, a physical dismissal of my words. "You'll be much happier now. You just need some time to adjust. I know what you saw upset you. I never intended to frighten you."

I can't hold back my bitter laugh. "Didn't you? You terrified me when you put on that skull mask and assaulted me in the dark. You threatened me with a knife."

"Just like you told me in your fantasies." He bites out the words, clearly agitated. "I acted out your deepest desires."

I breathe through my nose and suppress the urge to vomit.

He knows all of my secrets because he positioned himself as GentAnon.

"I confessed those fucked-up fantasies because I thought it was a safe space to express them. I thought I was talking to someone anonymous. Someone who understood me. I trusted you."

I told my illicit pen pal my most vulnerable secrets, and I'd felt secure in purging my inner darkness with him.

Instead, I made myself a target for a sadistic psychopath.

"How did you find my screenname?" I ask through numb lips.

My mind spins as I try to piece together what's happened to me. How long has Dane been watching me?

"You said we met at the bar before you came into the café for the first time. That was a few weeks before GentAnon messaged me. How did you find my erotica?"

He cracks an egg over the pan, a little too sharply. "You don't want to know that."

"Yes, I do," I insist, even though I really would prefer not to hear the sickening extent of his stalking.

But I have to understand him. I can't talk my way to freedom if I don't know everything about my situation.

"I've been watching over you ever since the night we met," he admits. "I think that much is obvious now."

"*Watching over me?*" I repeat, incredulous. "You mean *stalking me*."

His jaw tenses, but his movements are deft as he removes the cooked food from the pan. He places a full plate on the island in front of me, along with a glass of water.

Then he takes a knife and fork to cut my food into bite-sized pieces. He places the knife in the sink, well out of my reach.

Clearly, he's not going to tempt me with a potential weapon. Not after I attacked him with the heavy brass lamp almost as soon as I woke up from the drugs.

"Eat," he commands.

My stomach rumbles as the rich scent of bacon suffuses my senses. Even though I still feel queasy, I'm painfully aware of the fact that I haven't eaten in a full day. I have to keep my strength up and my wits sharp.

I take a bite of eggs. It tastes like ashes on my tongue, but I force myself to chew and swallow.

"Are you going to answer my question?" I press

when half my plate is empty. "How did you know to position yourself as GentAnon?"

"No." He takes a bite of his own bacon, and I realize he's not planning to say more.

"No, what?"

"No, I'm not going to answer your question."

I gape at him. "You owe me the truth, Dane."

His brow furrows, as though he's struggling to process my declaration. It occurs to me that he probably doesn't think he owes me anything. Judging by his puzzled expression, in his mind, he's never owed anything to anyone.

"You're upset," he says after a long moment. "I don't want to tell you when it will only make you more upset. I don't like how you're looking at me."

"And how am I looking at you? Like you're a monster who stalked and kidnapped me? Does that make you uncomfortable? Because I'm not remotely sorry."

I fix him with the full force of my defiant glower. I won't make this easy for him. If the way I look at him disturbs him, he'll be eager to let me go soon enough.

8

DANE

Two Months Ago

I straighten the painting on the freshly mounted hanger and then step back to check my work. The stormy sea is perfectly parallel with the top of the chest of drawers in my cramped little bedroom.

There's barely space in here for my king-size bed and a few basic furnishings, but I've made this ramshackle house comfortable enough. I finalized the cash sale three days ago, and I've spent the weekend setting up the bedroom. The rest of the house doesn't need to be furnished—it's best if it continues to appear uninhabited.

I don't want Abigail to get curious about her new neighbor. I plan to watch her from my garden across the street from her apartment building, and she'll never know I'm here.

My larger, grander house across town is much more comfortable than this aged home with its peeling, powder blue exterior. It's been vacant for some time, and the owners were all too eager to sell above market price without an inspection.

I still haven't decided how or when I'll approach her outside of our brief, daily meetings at the café. For now, I'm enjoying my clandestine study of my prey. Watching her is thrilling, fascinating like nothing I've ever experienced.

Earlier this afternoon, I acquired her painting—the first one I ever saw her paint. She has a modest stall at the market, and a clueless tourist bought the stormy beach scene.

The never would've appreciated the piece like I do.

So, I waited for them to leave the market and then purchased it from them. They didn't mind parting with the treasure for a measly hundred-dollar bill.

I sit back on my new bed and stare up at the painting. It deserves a far better display than the yellowing wallpaper in this dilapidated house, but for now, it will have to do.

In fact, if I acquire more of her art, I can conceal the cracks in the walls entirely.

I'll go back to the market next weekend and buy all of the paintings she sells to the appreciative tourists. They might enjoy her artistic style, but they're just looking for a pretty souvenir. I'm confident that my cash will be enough to convince them to hand over their purchases.

I love watching Abigail paint late into the night —especially her darker, erotic masterpieces—but the time she spends typing at her laptop is infuriating. I can't see what she's writing, and that's maddening.

Untenable.

I've formulated a plan to satisfy my burning curiosity. It's risky, but I can't deny that the risk is exhilarating.

I leave the bedroom and step out into the night. The street is quiet, and Abigail's window is dark. She's not home. I followed her to make sure of it almost an hour ago. It's half past nine, and she's at the dive bar where we first met.

The meeting she doesn't remember.

I force my tense jaw to relax. If I'd conquered Abigail in one night, I wouldn't experience this life-changing hunt. She frustrates me, but I can't deny that this is the most entertainment I've ever experienced when pursuing a beautiful woman. She doesn't know the game we're playing, but I'm enjoying it immensely.

When I take the first step across the empty street, all of my senses come alive in a way I've never known. I'm inside the ground floor breezeway of her building within seconds, tucked out of sight in the shadows.

My fingers shake slightly when I reach into my pocket, so I fist them around the lock picking kit I purchased online.

As a surgeon, I'm known for my steady hands. This anomaly is completely out of character, a novelty. Adrenaline hums through my veins, an almost giddy rush.

But there's no one around to witness my crime.

I won't be caught. I won't be caged.

Despite that knowledge, my body feels as though I might as well be skydiving rather than quietly breaking into her apartment.

My heart pounds against my ribcage when the

lock disengages, and her front door swings open with a rusty squeak. I can navigate the cramped space by the streetlight that filters through the large living room window; it would be stupid to turn on the lights.

No matter how I'm craving to study every detail of her home.

Curiosity nips at me, an insistent bite, but I force myself to focus on my goal: finding her laptop. I have to be smart about this, so I'll be in and out of her apartment as quickly as possible. There's no time to indulge myself in fully exploring her place.

I often see her writing while she's curled up on her couch, but it only takes a few seconds for me to ascertain that her laptop isn't there. She usually carries it with her into her bedroom once she's finished with her feverish, mysterious typing.

I cross the living room in a few long strides and enter her darkened bedroom.

My gaze skates over the small figurines that cover her dresser and the haphazard stacks of books overflowing from her nightstand. The temptation to study her trinkets and preferred literature is powerful enough to test my resolve. I take a breath and remind myself that I'm in control.

She fascinates me, but her allure isn't strong enough to compel my actions.

I risked this break-in for a single purpose, so I keep my focus on finding her laptop.

It's on the floor beside a stack of books, tucked halfway under the bed. Was she looking at something online late at night? Maybe she has a particular, perverted website she likes to visit.

I'll make sure to check her browser history as well as any personal documents she's written.

Any insight into her sexual preferences will help me seduce her. And if I'm right about her kinky predilections, I'll feel more secure showing her the darkest aspects of my cruel nature. There will be less risk involved if I know exactly what she wants me to do to her.

I set the laptop on the bed, which is an unmade tangle of sheets.

My lips twist with distaste. Abigail is untidy.

A bad habit I will have to break once she's mine.

I shake off the possessive thought and ignore the unease that stirs in my gut at how fiercely I want this woman.

The laptop instantly illuminates when I open it. A photo of the beach fills the screen, and a small icon with her face is framed in a circle at the center of the idyllic image. There's a text box just beneath it, the cursor flickering in a mocking rhythm.

Fuck.

It's password protected.

Her secrets are in my hands but hopelessly out of reach.

I narrow my eyes at the computer as though it's a particularly irksome enemy that I'm about to eviscerate. For a few long seconds, my fingers hover over the keyboard. I contemplate guessing her password.

But I have no idea if my attempts will be logged somehow. Even worse, I could end up locked out entirely. Abigail will definitely know someone has tampered with it if that happens.

She'll know someone was in her home while she was out.

She might call the police. There could be an investigation.

No, I can't try to guess her password. And I'm no hacker, even if I'm proficient with technology. It's a skill I've learned just like any other to progress my career, but I've never needed to learn how to break into a woman's private laptop.

My hands clench to fists just above the keyboard.

I'm going to have to leave unsatisfied.

The distinctive sound of a key scraping a lock

grates down my spine. Her front door creaks open, and my stomach drops.

Abigail is home early.

She was supposed to stay at the bar for at least another two hours. She usually indulges with her friends until nearly midnight when she goes out.

Fuck!

I've only been watching her for a few weeks. I was a fool to think I could fully learn her habits in that time. Abigail is quirky, difficult to pin down. I should've known that I couldn't rely on her to stick to any sort of schedule.

I quickly close the laptop, and my eyes can't quite adjust to the darkness in the absence of artificial light from the screen. Her soft footsteps pad across the living room. In less than three seconds, she'll enter her bedroom and find me here. She'll scream for help.

And I'll end up in a cage.

I grit my teeth and dive under her bed.

I will not go to prison.

Even if the prospect of hiding from her is somewhat preposterous. It feels intrinsically wrong to be cowering in the shadows, as though this delicate woman could pose any threat to me.

But I don't have a choice. I'll have to remain quiet

and hidden until I can slip out of her apartment without being noticed.

That might mean spending the entire night down here.

My fingernails dig into my palms, and I draw in a deep breath as quietly as I can manage.

Can she hear my heart hammering? My blood is pounding in my ears.

If I felt like I was skydiving before, now I'm in freefall without a parachute. The peril isn't just pretend anymore. If I'm caught...

I gnash my teeth and forcibly close off that line of thinking. Spiraling into anxiety won't help get me out of this farcical situation.

I can't do anything except remain still and draw in careful breaths. The adrenaline thrums through me, making my limbs shaky and my mind fizzy. It's terrifying and exhilarating in equal measure.

I've never experienced anything this powerful, and even though I'm losing control, I revel in the intense new emotions. Ensconced in darkness, I allow myself to sink into the fear-soaked physical responses, marveling at the way my breath shudders in and out of my tight lungs.

Even this existential dread is a gift only she can give me.

I can hardly wait for the day I feel the opposite. How visceral will my pleasure be when I finally claim her?

The prospect causes my muscles to coil in carnal anticipation, and to my shock, my cock begins to stiffen.

Before I can fully process the fact that I'm getting a hard-on, she turns on the bedside lamp. Then her soft cotton, periwinkle blue dress drops onto the hardwood floor, and I can no longer deny my erection.

Her panties drop next: pale pink cotton briefs.

I bite my tongue to hold back a hungry growl. The small rumble that manages to escape is mercifully smothered by the creaking of her aged mattress springs when she gets into bed.

Naked.

Right above me.

Her hand appears, fumbling at the floor just to the right of my head. I crane my neck to the side, and her long fingers nearly brush my hair before she feels the familiar shape of her laptop.

She picks it up, and the computer disappears along with her hand.

Damn it.

This can't be happening. I'm going to have to

listen to her typing whatever it is that absorbs her so completely, and I still won't have a clue what she's writing.

Within seconds, I hear the rapid tapping of her fingertips on the keyboard, but I remain completely ignorant. She's probably typing in her password, but there's no way to discern a pattern.

A few soft clicks. More tapping.

Faster now.

She blows out a long sigh, as though she's purging physical tension through her dainty fingers. The mattress shifts above me. She must be moving into a more comfortable position.

It shifts again.

The aged springs must be causing her discomfort, because she seems to be practically squirming in her sheets.

And still, she keeps typing.

Another sigh. Another shift.

My teeth are locked hard enough to make my jaw ache. A realization is dawning, but I don't want to acknowledge it.

My cock already seems to know exactly what's happening because it's painfully stiff in the confines of my jeans.

Then she stops typing, and her low moan flushes

the humid air with erotic heat. The movement of the mattress is undulating now, a regular, rolling rhythm.

No.

This can't be happening. The woman I've been lusting after for weeks is masturbating directly above me while I hide under her bed.

For an insane moment, I consider joining her on the bed. I could pin her down and clamp my hand over her mouth to muffle her pretty scream. She'd fight, but my other hand around her throat would be enough to subdue her. Those remarkable, aquamarine eyes would shine with tears even as they soften at the edge of losing consciousness.

She doesn't breathe unless I allow it. She doesn't speak unless it's to moan my name.

"Dane..."

My entire body locks up tight.

My dark fantasy of our mutual, twisted pleasure is all too visceral. I can't give in to temptation. She's not ready to accept me like that yet.

"Dane..."

It takes me several racing heartbeats to process the fact that I didn't just imagine her moaning my name.

Jesus Christ.

She's thinking about me while she pleasures herself.

She'll barely look at me when I'm at the café, but some part of her must remember our intense connection.

Abigail wants me.

My fist unfurls, and my fingers fumble at my belt. It's as though some irresistible compulsion has taken hold of my body, and even as I know this is madness, I free my aching cock. My sharp intake of breath is masked by her rapid panting and the squeaking of her mattress springs.

Pleasure shudders down my spine, and I bite the inside of my cheek to hold in a primal snarl of frustration and desire.

I should be inside her right now. The tight sheath of her cunt should be squeezing my dick, not my own fist. She should be weeping and begging me for release.

"Dane!"

She cries out my name, and for the first time in my life, I lose control of my body entirely. Ecstasy overtakes me in a vicious wave, dragging me to completion against my will. Cum sears my hand, and my cheeks heat with pleasure and a hint of shame.

Unease twists my gut as I crash back down from my cruel high. The power this fragile woman holds over me isn't just thrilling; it's shaking my entire worldview.

I close my eyes and draw in a deep breath at the same time as she sighs in contentment.

Abigail will pay for this. She'll crawl to me on her hands and knees and apologize with her mouth. Only when I'm satisfied that she's thoroughly humbled and completely desperate for me, I'll finally allow her the mercy of an orgasm.

The savage thought is almost hot enough to stir my lust again, but for now, I'm spent.

The mattress dips, and her hand appears again as she returns her laptop to its place beneath her bed.

My mind whirs. I have to know what she was writing that got her so aroused. For weeks, I've watched her cheeks turn a lovely shade of pink while she's typing. Now I know for sure that she's getting herself off with whatever it is that she writes.

Does she write about me? Is that why she moaned my name?

I formulate a daring plan to discover her secrets. I've risked breaking into her apartment once. I can do it again.

After I borrow her laptop for the day.

Someone in Charleston will know how to unlock it without her password. My money will ensure that any qualms about hacking will be alleviated.

Then I can return the infuriating device to her bedroom, and she'll never know it was missing.

Satisfied with my course of action, I finally allow myself to relax. As I listen to the sound of her deep, even breaths, I follow Abigail into sleep.

9

ABIGAIL

Now

"Fine," Dane bites out, green eyes blazing. "You want to know how I became Gent-Anon? I borrowed your laptop and found your erotica."

I gape at him. "*Borrowed?* You mean you stole it. How? When?"

His gaze cuts away for an instant before snapping back to mine. "I went into your apartment and found your laptop two months ago. Is that what you want to hear?"

"You *went in?*" I press, forcing him to confront the

softer language he's selecting over the harsh truth. "So, you broke into my home more than once."

"I told you that you don't want to hear this." He says it like I'm the unreasonable one.

I narrow my eyes at him. "Oh, I absolutely do. I want *you* to hear it. Listen to how crazy this is. How can you expect me to love you after everything you've done to me?"

He glares at me with open defiance. "Everything I've done has been for you. I had to make sure you truly wanted me. The first night we met—the night you don't remember—you told me you wanted to be overpowered. Forced. I had to know that was real before I acted out the dark fantasy that we share. Both of us, Abigail. You wanted everything that I offered you. Or have you forgotten how many orgasms I gave you?"

My fingers shake with the rage that rushes through my system, so I curl them into fists. "You know I orgasm when a man forces himself on me. I told you what happened with Tom on the night of my debutante ball. How he did it again and again, and how ashamed I felt for letting it happen. You assaulted me, Dane."

His head jerks to the side in a staunch refusal of my accusation. "You're not thinking clearly," he says roughly. "I am nothing like him. I protect you from men like him. Just like I protected you from your neighbor, Ron."

The memory of Dane's blood-splattered face flashes across my mind. He'd said he was going to talk to Ron, and he returned covered in mud and blood.

"What did you do to him?" I ask, breathless with dawning horror.

Dark brows draw together in forbidding slashes. "I made sure he'll never touch you again."

"What does that mean?" I demand, voice going shrill despite my efforts to remain calm and rational.

"It means I'll do what's necessary to keep you safe," he snaps back, his composure slipping too. "This conversation is over."

"I don't think so," I hiss. "You don't get to tell me when to shut up. You don't control me. Not anymore."

He scowls. "I never tried to control you. How many times do I have to tell you that I want you just as you are? I expect obedience when we fuck because that's what we both like. We're perfectly compatible."

"You're delusional."

His face goes cold again, his eyes unnervingly calculating.

"I won't entertain this conversation further. Rail at me if you want. Get it out of your system. But I'm no longer participating."

I clench my jaw shut to hold in a scream of impotent rage. Shouting at him will get me nowhere. He seems convinced that I'm hysterical, irrational. After he stalked and kidnapped me.

Playing into his characterization of my behavior will only make him more convinced that he's right to hold me here against my will.

I watch in stony silence as he takes the plates to the sink. The dishes clatter a bit more loudly than necessary as he cleans up, tension clear in every taut line of his powerful body. And yet, he manages to carry out the chore with a completely blank expression.

He doesn't ask for my help as he dries the pans and puts everything neatly back in its place.

Something about the domesticity of the situation brings his psychopathy into sharp relief. He's holding me against my will, but instead of using violence to subdue me, he's cooking and cleaning for me. As though I'm a guest rather than his captive.

He truly thinks I'll just get over his heinous

crimes against me. He's acting as though we can be together like a normal couple.

If anything, he's doting on me. In his twisted mind, he probably thinks that he's seeing to my every need.

He's incapable of understanding that what I need more than anything is to get away from him.

"Come with me," he commands when the kitchen is spotless. "I have something for you."

I cross my arms over my chest. "I don't want it."

His lips press to a grim line. "You'll accept it regardless. You don't seem ready to accept the fact that you don't have to work anymore to make ends meet. I'm going to show you how I will provide for you. You'll learn to embrace it, even if you have always been stubborn about accepting what my money can afford us. That ends now."

I never should've let him buy my drinks. I shouldn't have accepted the fancy dress for Meadows' wedding.

I'd been afraid that he'd wield his wealth as a weapon against me, just like my family.

I'd been right, but I hadn't listened to my gut instincts.

My back goes ramrod straight.

"I told you that I won't be controlled financially

ever again." It takes effort to maintain a calm, flat tone. "Whatever you have for me, I refuse to accept. You can't buy my affection, Dane."

He shakes his head sharply, the only sign that his irritation is breaking through his cold façade.

"This isn't about controlling you. It never has been. I want to take care of you. You're the one who's insisting on misunderstanding what I'm offering. I will never leverage my money against you. What I provide doesn't come with strings attached."

"No, you're misunderstanding." He truly seems to believe what he's saying. "You want to keep me captive. You think I'll soften toward you if you buy me things and ensure my comfort. That's controlling behavior, Dane. You have to see that."

"I will provide for you, Abigail. This isn't a negotiation. And it's not a manipulation. I told you from the beginning that I'm selfish. This is what I want: you, content and cared for in the way that you deserve. In time, I'll prove to you that I don't expect anything in return."

His eyes glitter with icy determination. "Now, are you going to come with me, or am I going to have to carry you?"

I fix him with an imperious stare that's icy

enough to match his. "I don't intend to be spanked like an unruly child again. I'll walk."

He shrugs. "It's your choice."

I hold back the tirade that it's not a choice at all. He will take me wherever he wants to go, despite my protests. My only autonomy in this situation is whether or not I maintain some semblance of dignity.

He turns his back on me and strides out of the kitchen. It's a small mercy that he didn't reach for me, but I don't dare hesitate to follow him in case he changes his mind about touching me.

We go through the labyrinthine rooms again, making our way back to the cavernous, wood-paneled entry hall. He silently leads me up the grand staircase, and I realize we're heading toward his bedroom.

My steps falter. "I'm not going to have sex with you, if that's what you're thinking."

His shoulders stiffen, but he doesn't turn to face me when he replies, "I'm not taking you to my bedroom." He opens one of the doors we passed on our way down the long corridor with the portraits. "I converted this guest room into a studio for you while you were sleeping."

I hate the longing that tugs at my heart, even as

my stomach churns. Dane knows my deepest dreams of being a successful artist, and he's using them against me.

"If you think I'll want you just because you've provided a space for me to paint, you're mistaken. This isn't a gift, Dane. It's a betrayal."

He finally turns to face me, pivoting in the center of the room, just beside the easel he's already set up alongside a table of paints.

"I'll tolerate your barbed comments because I appreciate the fact that the way I pursued you was unconventional. If you would take a moment to see things from my perspective, perhaps you wouldn't be so prickly."

I lift my brows, incredulous. "And what is your perspective? What mental gymnastics have you done to justify all of this?"

He lifts one finger. "You were so drunk that you forgot our initial meeting, so I couldn't ask you out." He lifts a second finger before I can respond. "You refused to make eye contact when I came into the café, but I knew you wanted me." A third finger goes up. "We both have dark, kinky fantasies that defy social norms. I had to be sure that you really wanted what I had to offer before I risked showing you my true self."

I cross my arms over my chest. "You're right. You are selfish. Everything you're describing is about what you want, about keeping you safe from judgment. You could've been vulnerable with me. You could have put yourself on the line and asked me out on a date. I should've had the chance to truly choose you, but you took that away from me. Everything we've shared has been a lie, a manipulation to get me into your bed."

He waves his arms at the room in a jerky gesture. "Getting you into my bed would've been easy. Does this look like seduction to you? I'm offering you everything you could ever want. I'll offer you the world, Abigail. And I've offered you myself in return. My real, frightening, unmasked self. You saw what I am at my core, and you wept in ecstasy."

It finally registers that he must think he's made himself vulnerable. He keeps saying that he's revealed his true self to me in a way he's never shown anyone.

But that doesn't make him any less monstrous.

I just couldn't see him clearly before. I didn't have all the horrific facts to make a rational assessment of him.

"Just because it's not carnal doesn't mean it's not a form of seduction," I inform him. "You're trying to lure me in with every word, every tender action. Even offering me this studio is part of a twisted game to you. But you can't trick me into loving you again. I don't think I ever did love you, because I didn't know you at all. I loved an idea of you, but that man was never real."

His eyes turn stormy, and I know I've said the wrong thing.

"If you're feeling so emotional, I'm sure some time at your easel will help." He speaks in clipped tones, and his massive body seems even larger than usual as all of his powerful muscles flex with barely restrained aggression.

I take a wary step back, refusing to enter the studio with the beast. "Dane..."

"You will paint, Abigail."

"You can't compel my art." I swallow hard against my rising fear. "That's not how it works."

"I've seen your real masterpieces," he reveals coldly, no longer bothering to hide behind charm and beguilement. "The dark, erotic paintings that you keep hidden in your closet. But you don't have to hide your talent anymore."

The reminder that he's broken into my apartment multiple times makes bile burn at the back of my throat.

"Those are private," I choke out.

"Not from me. Any secrets you think you have, I know them. I know *you*. All of you. And I choose every part of you. I won't apologize for wanting you."

"That much has become clear," I reply bitterly. "I won't hold my breath for an apology."

He doesn't feel a shred of remorse for what he's done to me, for the countless violations that I can't even begin to fathom.

"Paint," he commands.

"No."

He can't make me. He could crush his fist around mine and force me to lift a brush to the waiting canvas, but he can't compel me to create art. My tumultuous emotions are my own to purge through my paintings. That part of me will never belong to anyone else. Certainly not the man who's betrayed me on a level I never thought possible.

"Abigail..." My name is a warning, but I refuse to heed it.

"I won't do it. I won't paint for you."

His brows draw together, forbidding. "You can come in willingly, or I can put you here." He points to the chair that's set up in front of the easel, presumably for my comfort. "If you won't do it for me, do it for yourself. You need this."

"You don't know what I need!" I fling the defiant words at him, losing my composure. "I need to get away from you. I need my freedom."

"I've set you free," he growls. "You just don't want to listen."

Rage curls my fists at my sides, and suddenly, I'm surging toward him.

"You want me to come to you like a trained pet?" I rail at him. "You think I'll roll over and do what you say?"

The canvas is in my hands, and I hurl it at his beautiful face.

"Fuck you!"

He bats the canvas away at the last second, and it clatters to the parquet floor. His lips peel back from his teeth in an animal snarl, and he lunges for me.

A defiant scream tears from my chest, and I grab the table where the paints have been neatly arranged for me. It's lightweight enough that I'm able to lift it, and I raise the delicate antique like an unwieldy bat. In a split second, I swing.

But he's too fast. Too strong.

He lifts one corded arm just in time to stop the impact to his head. He barks out a rough shout as the table splinters against his shoulder, and I'm not sure if it's a sound of pain or a predator's warning.

I lunge for the easel, desperate for another weapon.

Arguing was futile. My rationality is gone. His insane refusals to listen to reason have driven me to a purely primal, enraged state.

I'm not sure if I'm fighting to get away from him, or if some savage part of me just wants to inflict a fraction of the damage he's caused me. I want him to feel the pain that's shredding my heart. I know now that he's incapable of that kind of emotional agony, so I'll wound him physically.

His arm loops around my waist just as my fingers brush the easel, and he drags me back before I can fully grasp it. He tackles me with his full weight, and we're both falling.

At the last instant, he turns his body so that he catches the brunt of the impact with the hardwood floor.

I shriek and writhe in his arms, but he rolls on top of me, quickly pinning me so that I'm face-down beneath him. My hands scramble for purchase, and my palms slip in something wet.

I've fallen on the canvas that I threw at him, and several paint tubes have been squashed under us. Blue splatter becomes a sapphire smear under my hands as I continue to struggle like a wild thing.

"That's it," he rumbles at my ear. "Fight me like you've always wanted to. Like you really mean it."

I scream again, a sound of pure fury. I've never meant anything more in my life than my desire to hurt him now.

His left hand is beside my scrabbling fingers, sliding in the paint so that his palm is coated in blue. His other fists in my hair, drawing my head back sharply to further restrict my struggles. Then he caresses my cheek, and the paint is warm on his broad palm. It slides over one side of my face, covering me from my brow to my jaw.

His grip on my hair shifts, forcibly tilting my head to the side and shoving me forward. My cheek presses against the canvas, marking it with my twisted expression of fear and impotent rage. I shriek and jerk in his cruel hold, but all I manage to do is spread more paint in manic swaths.

"I want an imprint of your pretty scream," he says, voice rough with desire. "I'll admire this masterpiece later. We both will."

I can't find the air to tell him that he's insane. My lungs seize, and my chest draws tight enough to crush my heart.

My fists pound the canvas, sending sprays of blue droplets flying.

"This is what you've always wanted." He says it like encouragement rather than a condemnation. "You want to know the difference between me and the men who violated you? Your body already knows. When they touched you, you shut down and surrendered. But with me, you fight back. You feel safe enough to challenge me because you know I won't truly hurt you."

"You are hurting me!" I wail, an agonized truth drawn deep from my soul.

No one has ever hurt me like this.

Because what he's saying makes some perverse sort of sense, and I can't accept it. If it's true, I'm just as crazy as he is. Just as fucked up.

He thinks I'm perfect for him, but that can't be real. I can't let it be real.

The prospect that I was destined to satisfy a heartless monster is too disgusting to process. I've always known that something is deeply wrong with me, but the Dane I loved made me feel like I could embrace every part of myself. Indulging in my dark desires had become empowering.

But I've never been more powerless than I am now.

"No, I'm not." He refuses to acknowledge that

he's hurting me in the worst way. "I won't so much a leave a bruise on you to prove it."

Tears leak from my eyes, diluting the paint beneath my cheek.

"When you shared your fantasies with me online, you shared your true self," he reasons. "If I hadn't found your screen name, you never would've trusted me with your secrets in person. You want to know why I couldn't simply ask you out at the café? This was the best way. The only way. By the time you agreed to a date, I already knew exactly what you wanted. You wouldn't have opened up to me enough to sign our contract if I hadn't positioned myself as GentAnon. I have no regrets, Abigail. This is how it had to be between us. I will fulfill your every forbidden desire."

"I don't want you to," I counter in a ragged whisper. "Let me go."

"No. Not until you accept the truth of what we are, what we share. I'm not letting you leave this room until you scream my name while you orgasm."

"No," I moan in pure horror.

My revulsion is that much more acute because I'm starting to realize that the warmth flooding my veins isn't simply white-hot rage. Desire pulses between my legs, and my nipples are hard buds.

He keeps his firm grip on my hair with one hand while the other dips between my chest and the canvas.

"Hush now, pet," he soothes, dropping a tender kiss on my nape. "No more arguing. I don't want to hear another word unless it's my name on your pretty lips."

I want to defy him, to continue railing at him. But my screams stick in my constricted throat, and I can't manage more than a garbled groan.

It sounds unbearably erotic, and he drops another doting kiss on my exposed neck.

My cheeks flush with shame, and my clit pulses in response.

In this moment, I hate myself. I hate *him.*

His paint slicked hand wedges beneath me, sliding under the neckline of my dress to cup my breast. The pressure is uncomfortable, but the bite of pain makes my nipple throb where it's crushed against his palm. He squeezes gently, and I gasp into the canvas. I'm writhing, and I tell myself it's because I'm still trying to escape.

But my struggles only fuel my lust, just like in all of the terrible, forbidden fantasies I so foolishly shared with him.

"Dane..." His name is a whimper, a plea.

"Better," he praises. "But I want you to scream for me."

His other, unpainted hand finally releases my hair, but his bulky frame is heavy enough to keep me pinned. He traces the shape of my body with something like reverence, coveting every inch of me. When his fingertips skim my thigh, I tense.

"You're safe with me, little dove," he soothes. "Submit."

I choke on a sob, and pleasure sizzles through me when he pinches my nipple. He tugs and torments it in the exact way I like. He knows his clever ministrations will make me come undone.

My body uncoils for him even as my heart hammers against my ribcage like a trapped bird.

His fingers skate up my thigh, easing my dress up to expose my ass. They dip between my legs, and he releases a low, satisfied hum at the slick arousal he finds there.

Mortification sears my cheeks when I realize that I've never been so wet.

He was right: he's unleashed something dark inside me that craves this cruelty, the struggle and forced submission.

"So soft and ready for me," he says with rough desire. "Is your sensitive little clit aching?"

"Don't..." I choke on the plea before I can fully verbalize it.

He shushes me again. "Only my name, remember?"

His fingers brush my clit, and I buck beneath him as stars burst across my vision at the punch of pleasure.

"Don't worry, pet. I'm not going to fuck you now. I won't break you."

The ragged sound that heaves from my chest is somewhere between a maddened laugh and a sob.

No, Dane doesn't want to risk breaking his precious pet. He said he wants all of me, and that seems to mean that he wants my mind intact.

How can he not see that he's destroying my soul with every tender touch and soft word of praise?

With every masterful brush of his hands over my most sensitive areas, I feel the caresses of the man I loved, the man I trusted with my whole heart. The fact that a monster is holding me instead is exquisite agony. My body welcomes the pain of his cruel fingers pinching my nipples, smearing paint over my breasts like I'm his most passionate work of art.

And my core is molten for him, my inner muscles contracting around nothing as he toys with my clit. I'm aching to be filled, but there's nothing I dread more than the prospect of his cock inside me.

He promised not to fuck me, but that doesn't mean this isn't a violation.

It's just like the night he attacked me as the masked man.

He hadn't taken his own pleasure in my body on that night, either. But I understand now that his carnal satisfaction was far more sadistic than simple physical release. Forcing orgasms from my reluctant body seems to please him on a primal, perverted level that only a complete psychopath could understand.

I can feel his thick erection pressing into my upper thigh. He's getting off on this: the control over me, my helplessness to stop my body from responding to him.

I'm on the cusp of the most powerful orgasm of my life. Pleasure coils low in my belly, and I thrash against the wet canvas. I fear that I'm no longer struggling to get away; I'm desperately seeking more stimulation. My clit is painfully hard as he teases around it in maddening circles. His low, arrogant laugh dances up my spine like a caress, and I shudder at the answering rush of pleasure that washes through me in a warm wave.

"Come for me, pet."

He slides two thick fingers inside me and crooks them against my most sensitive spot. At the same time, his thumb presses down on my clit.

My orgasm rips through me, and I scream in ecstasy and despair. I'm helpless to resist the bliss that shreds my psyche as it rakes through my body. My inner muscles contract around his fingers, clamping down hard to keep him inside me. The release goes on and on. Sheet lighting flashes over my vision, and I'm a whimpering mess, writhing on the horrific, perverted painting we're making together.

"That was very pretty, but you forgot something," he admonishes, continuing to wring ruthless pleasure from my core. "My name, Abigail. Say it."

"Please..." I can't. The surrender would be too shameful to bear. He has to allow me this last shred of my dignity, my autonomy.

"You'll get no mercy from me, pet."

His fingers finally withdraw from my pulsing pussy, but before I can heave in a gasp of relief, his touch trails upward.

I try to wriggle my way free, but his other hand releases my breasts to grip my ass cheek. His fingers dig into my flesh in a warning bite, spreading me wide open for him.

"You're mine," he declares. "Every part of you."

His desire-slicked finger presses against my asshole, and I try to buck away. He holds me steady, keeping me trapped for his amusement.

"You will submit, Abigail. Surrender."

"Dane. Please, Dane..." I'm babbling, repeating his name like that will earn his mercy.

But he has none.

"You'll have to come for me," he coaxes. "Come for me while I finger your tight little asshole, and I'll relent."

Something breaks inside me.

I don't have a choice. My mind accepts that my only way to escape this horrific ecstasy is to comply. And even if I didn't acknowledge that awful truth, my body would comply anyway.

Pleasure gathers low in my belly as his finger slips inside me. I clench around him, but my final efforts to resist him only awaken forbidden sensations I've never experienced before.

He bites out a curse and pushes deeper. "I'll stretch this virgin asshole with my cock soon enough. But I'll get you ready for me before I claim you. I'll never harm you, little dove."

I close my eyes and turn my face into the canvas, as though I can hide from what's happening to me. My body softens, and he begins to pump his finger into me in gentle thrusts.

"Good girl," he praises. "Such a sweet pet."

A strangled sound catches in my throat, a carnal groan. My core throbs with desire in response to his praise, and my clit pulses in time with my racing heartbeat.

He torments me with slow, terrible pleasure as he continues to toy with my ass, teasing me until I fully surrender. I'm not trying to squirm away from him anymore. Heat flushes my skin, and I practically pant with mounting lust.

"You're going to come for me just like this." His voice has dropped to a deeper register, and he sounds almost drunk on his power over me. "I'm not going to touch your pretty cunt or your hard little clit. Only this."

His darkly perverse command shudders through me, and I weep into the messy painting we've made. The pleasure is so keen that it cuts my heart like a knife. My core is swollen and achy, as though his gentle fingers have marked me with bruises deep inside my pussy.

But, true to his word, he hasn't harmed me physically.

My soul is another matter entirely.

Ecstasy gathers low in my belly, and all of my muscles coil tight in anticipation of release. Sweat slicks my skin, and soft moans leave my chest with every heaving breath.

"Let go," he urges. "Give me everything."

I come apart on a scream, and his name echoes through the studio he's provided for me.

"Good girl." His warm praise layers over my sharp cry, and he pumps his fingers into me, drawing out my orgasm.

My scream melts into a sob, and I shake beneath him. I'm utterly spent and shattered beyond repair.

Dane commanded me to paint for him, and despite my refusal, he's compelled me to make a shameful, carnal work of art.

10

DANE

One Month Ago

I've been messaging Abigail as GentAnon for several agonizingly long weeks. Meanwhile, she only exchanges rote pleasantries with me at the café every morning.

I know her deepest, darkest secrets, but she acts like she barely knows me.

She doesn't realize that I've learned more about her than she'd ever divulge if I approached her as charming, "normal" Dr. Dane Graham.

I'm so close to claiming her.

But I have to be absolutely certain of our chemistry. I have to prove to her that she craves these twisted games. When I do finally approach her, she'll be ready to accept our connection.

And I'm tired of keeping things virtual. All those nights alone in my bed while exchanging dirty desires with her have made me restless. The imbalance of power chafes at my pride. I would do anything to possess her, but she barely acknowledges my existence.

I'll prove to her how deep my devotion goes. I'll give her everything she wants, and she'll realize that she can be her true, unmasked self around me.

Just like I crave to share all of myself with her.

My civilized mask has never felt so heavy, a burden that I no longer want to bear.

It's past time for me to make my move in person. I've acquired enough knowledge to seduce her in exactly the way she craves.

My hunting knife is sheathed at my belt, and the appropriately intimidating skull mask is securely in my fist. Abigail wants to be frightened. I wonder how wet she'll get for me when she realizes her helplessness to resist the pleasure I'll wring from her fragile body.

Just the thought is enough to make me hard, so I take a breath and struggle to master my rising lust.

I'm hidden in the shadows of the breezeway to her building, and I'm further concealed by my head-to-toe black clothing.

Appropriately intimidating.

This is her final test, the last night I'll spend without her in my bed.

I'm not stupid enough to give away my identity, though. Until I know how she'll react, I can't risk her knowing who I am.

I've swapped out my usual expensive scent for a cheap, heavy amber cologne. And I can do a convincing enough American accent that she won't recognize my gravelly voice. The leather gloves are for sensory stimulation—the implication that I don't want to leave fingerprints heightens the sense of erotic danger.

It's a shame that I won't be able to feel her bare skin against mine, but I can forego that desire to fulfil this fantasy for her. There will be plenty of time for me to touch and explore at my leisure soon.

I'm practiced at picking the lock on her front door now. It only takes a few seconds to gain clandestine entry to her apartment.

I close the door behind me and lean back against the wall. I'll trap her as soon as she steps inside.

There will be no hiding under her bed this time,

no losing control of my physical responses. Tonight is about her pleasure, her acceptance.

I can wait to bury my cock in her wet cunt. She'll be begging me to claim her once I ask her out tomorrow. I've waited this long; I can manage one more day.

I don't plan to reveal my participation in this scene until I'm sure she'll understand. But until the day she's ready to hear it, I'll keep her completely satisfied and blissfully content.

And that means both of us will finally embrace our mutual darkness without shame or hesitation. We can be our true selves together.

This is a gift only I can give her. One day, she'll thank me for it.

"GOOD MORNING, ABIGAIL." I greet her warmly at the café, and it takes effort to keep the anticipatory, predatory edge from my charming smile.

"Hi." It's a soft, breezy reply: her usual polite demeanor.

She steams milk with one hand, and the other briefly touches her silly badges—a nervous habit that I've come to find endearing. Her smile is as sunny as ever, but she still refuses to look directly at me.

"Sorry," she says, "it'll be about a five-minute wait for your Americano. We're really busy this morning."

I nod in easy agreement. I've become used to the bitter taste of the espresso, and I look forward to the daily black Americanos she makes for me.

I'll make coffee for her tomorrow morning when she wakes up in my bed. I wonder how she takes it. Probably with copious heaps of sugar. Abigail does love her sweet drinks.

I'm watching her with more intensity than usual, willing her to make eye contact.

But she keeps her focus on her work. There's something strange about her this morning, something strained about her smile. As she grinds the espresso for my drink, her lovely lips go slack, and her rosy cheeks are chalky.

She seems to move on autopilot as she places a finished flat white onto the counter in front of me—freshly prepared with pretty swan latte art for the customer before me.

"Abigail?" I prompt, concern deepening my tone. "Are you all right?"

She remains fixated on the swan, and she doesn't answer me.

Her oddly blank expression disturbs me in a way I've never experienced before. My stomach dips, and my jaw tightens.

Boldly, I brush my fingers over the back of her hand to call her attention to me. I've never touched her at the café before, but something is wrong. I'm drawn to comfort my fragile little dove.

She gasps and yanks her hand away as though my touch has burned her. The jerky movement sends the flat white flying, and coffee splatters my crisp white shirt.

I can't hold back a sharp curse at her sudden withdrawal, her rejection. I've wanted her for so long, and she's cringing away from me.

"I'm so sorry!" She frantically turns to grab a clean cloth and rounds the espresso bar.

I stand in stunned silence for a full five seconds while she tries to blot away the brown stain on my shirt.

Abigail is touching me.

It's the first time she's willingly made contact with me since the night we met at the bar months ago. The rush of vicious, possessive pleasure is strong enough to make my muscles tighten like I'm under some invisible strain.

"I'm so sorry," she repeats, delicate hands fluttering around my torso.

I can't hold back any longer. I have to touch her again.

But she's on edge about something this morning, so I force my fingers to remain gentle as I encircle her slender wrists. Her pulse races in response to our visceral connection. She must feel it too.

She wants this. She wants *me.*

I've known she desires me ever since she moaned my name while I hid under her bed. But the reality of her lust for me is heady enough to make me almost drunk on pleasure.

Those clear, stunning aqua eyes meet mine, and she goes utterly still.

"It's fine," I soothe.

But she doesn't calm. Her pulse remains elevated, and she doesn't seem to be drawing in full breaths. Her cheeks are still far too pale for my liking.

"It's okay," I reassure her. "Breathe, Abigail."

"Oh my god, Dane!" Abigail's colleague, Stacy, rudely interrupts the intense moment we're sharing. "Are you all right?"

"It's just coffee." I shrug, eager to be rid of her irritating presence. "I have time to change before work."

The last is meant for Abigail. She still seems distressed about the mishap.

I've been holding her wrists for too long. It will seem inappropriate if I maintain the tender contact, so I force myself to withdraw.

Her arms drop to her sides, and her shoulders slump like she's barely keeping herself upright.

"Look at me, Abigail," I command. I can't stand how upset she is. Not on the day I anticipated her giddy excitement about our date tonight.

Her eyes snap to mine, and I keep her locked in my steady stare, anchoring her to me.

"It's all right," I promise again. I don't want her to think I'm angry with her.

"But I might've burned you," she protests.

I can't resist an arrogant smirk. "I've had worse than anything you could throw at me."

The idea that this delicate woman could every truly harm me is amusing. And it's rather adorable that she's so concerned about my well-being.

"But your shirt—"

"I have another one at work that I was going to wear after the gym." I cut her off before she can spiral into anxiety over the mistake. "If you want to make it up to me, you can agree to go to dinner with me."

Her pretty lips part, and for a moment, I anticipate her eager acceptance.

But she remains utterly quiet, and her breaths turn shallow again. Her eyes are still on mine, but her gaze is unfocused. The ground seems to shift under my feet, throwing me off-balance.

This isn't going at all to plan.

"Abby?" I forgot Stacy's presence until she speaks again. "You don't look so good. If you're sick, you need to go home."

Abigail isn't going anywhere until she agrees to a date with me.

"Come on," I cajole. "Let's get some fresh air."

I gently grasp her elbow, and she allows me to guide her outside. She barely seems aware that I'm touching her. Those lovely eyes remain unfocused, and her brow is furrowed with some mysterious worry.

Once we step out into the sunlight, she closes her eyes and finally draws in a deep breath. When she opens them again, her gaze is clearer, but guarded in a way I don't understand.

Maybe I'm making her uncomfortable with my persistent physical contact.

But she moaned my name while she masturbated. She wants me.

I just need to break through her shyness and proper Southern belle façade.

I skim my fingers up her arm, enjoying the way her creamy skin pebbles with awareness of my touch. Then I rest my hand on her shoulder, grounding her to me.

Something—or someone—at work has upset her this morning. That must be why she's behaving so strangely.

Whoever inflicted this distress will suffer for it. She'll give me a name eventually. I'll coax it out of her once the color returns to her cheeks.

"Breathe, Abigail." I don't like that she's so wary around me. I have to calm her down and make sure she knows she's safe with me. "Just breathe."

Pleasure suffuses my chest when she obeys.

"Why do you call me that?" she asks when she exhales.

"It's your name, isn't it?"

She gestures at her name badge that's pinned to her apron. "Everyone calls me Abby."

The fact that she doesn't remember our initial

meeting grates at me, but I manage a charming smile. "I suppose I'm still a bit more formal than the locals. Bad habit from back home."

I don't tell her that I'm the only one who will call her *Abigail.* That privilege is mine and mine alone.

"You're from England, right?" she asks.

I nod. We've never spoken about my accent at the café. I'm happy to share more personal information with her now, even if the topic is a bit mundane.

"From York originally. The old York."

"Oh. What brought you to South Carolina?"

My smile turns indulgent. These are topics to cover on our date later.

"You don't have to make small talk with me, Abigail." I savor her name on my tongue. "How are you feeling?"

She blinks. "Better, thanks."

She seems almost surprised.

"Good. Are you feeling well enough to go out to dinner with me tonight?"

"What?"

"You heard me," I say with teasing admonishment. "Have dinner with me."

Her refusal isn't an option, so I don't bother to soften the command into a question this time.

My fingers tighten on her shoulder ever so

slightly, and I barely suppress the urge to pull her closer.

Her willowy body goes rigid, and her eyes slide out of focus again.

Fuck.

Who upset her so deeply that she's completely distracted from the intense connection we share? The one I sealed last night when she came all over my gloved hand?

She reels back, breaking free of my careful hold on her shoulder.

"I can't," she blurts, gaze cutting away from mine. "I'm sorry."

"Abigail!" I call after her, but she's already ducking back into the café.

I rake a hand through my hair.

What the hell just happened?

11

DANE

Now

Over time, it became clear to me that Abigail wasn't anywhere near ready to accept the fact that I'm the masked man who broke into her apartment. After she finally opened up to me about how she was raped by that fucker, Tom, I knew it was too soon to reveal the truth. Then Ron attacked her, and she was so distressed.

Even though she experienced intense pleasure when I forced her to orgasm under the threat of my knife, she hadn't fully embraced the darkest aspects of our connection. And when we fucked, she'd struggled in bed a few times, but she hadn't truly fought me.

Until she was ready to indulge in those darkest games, I knew it was too soon to tell her that I was the masked man.

But then she broke into my second home and found the skull mask in my nightstand, and the choice was no longer mine. She'd been horrified.

But after what we just shared, she'll understand.

In her new studio, we fully realized the powerful eroticism of dancing at the edge of consent. The sensual painting that we created is proof of that. Later, we'll both admire it.

But for now, she's shaking and spent. And she's covered in paint.

I gather her up in my arms and hug her to my chest. As I carry her out of the studio, I marvel at the stunning woman who belongs to me, irrevocably and completely. Her creamy skin is still flushed from her orgasms, a deeper shade of pink coloring her chest and cheeks. The lovely hue blends with the blue paint that I stroked onto her body like she's my own personal canvas. I'll never be an artist like Abigail, but she's my masterpiece.

I take my time carrying her to my bedroom,

admiring my work. It'll be a shame to wash the paint away, so I etch the memory of her perfection into my mind.

She's *mine.*

I knew it was only a matter of time before she accepted our bond, my claim over her. She's been thorny since she woke up this morning, but now she looks serene. Subdued.

Her eyes are closed, and her breaths are deep and even. Her long, dark lashes fan her cheeks like a sleeping princess in one of her favorite animated musicals. That enchanting freckle on her cheekbone marks her as a unique, proud woman. I sensed it in her when I first laid eyes on her. Even then, my need to possess her completely had been inevitable.

My chest aches just looking at her. I want her so badly that my craving consumes me. My cock is still hard, but I have enough self-control to spare her from my selfish lust. There will be time for that later. She needed pleasure first.

I was right to seduce her in the studio. It served as a reminder of how good it can be between us.

Her accusations of stalking and kidnapping had stung a bit—as had the shocking blows with the lamp and the table—but I'm confident that I've done nothing wrong. She just didn't understand why I had to do everything that I've done to win her heart.

I meant what I said to her. It was the only way.

This is how it has to be between us: raw and dark and real.

Our connection is the only thing that matters to me now, the only real thing in my world.

She is my world.

My Abigail.

My sweet pet, my little dove.

All mine.

I step into my ensuite bathroom and carry her toward the bathtub. She's almost completely limp in my arms, so I carefully crouch down to turn on the water while I keep her in a firm hold. When I'm satisfied with the temperature, I ease off her dress and set her down so that she's reclining in the bath.

She's so still, and she allows me to position her like a doll.

My stomach knots.

What happened to my fierce pet who fought me with all her might? She should be looking at me with a lazy smile and utter devotion shining in her gemstone eyes.

"Abigail." Her name rasps from my tight throat.

She doesn't respond in any way. Her cheeks

remain rosy from her orgasms and the heat of the rising water, but her expression is frozen.

I cup warm water in my hand and carefully wash the paint from her heartbreaking face.

It's not only her beauty that's making my chest ache now. There's a dull throb in my heart with each heavy beat.

"Abigail." Her name is almost a growl this time, a warning that demands her attention.

"What do you want, Dane?" The question is soft and flat.

She sounded like this when she first woke up in my arms this morning. I'd thought she was woozy from the lingering drugs. Now, I don't know what to think. I don't know how to interpret this strange mood.

"I want you to look at me."

Her eyes open, and they instantly shine with fresh tears. They mingle with the warm water as I wash the last of the paint from her cheek.

"You're okay," I soothe her. I suppose our scene in the studio was intense. Some residual emotion is understandable. "Stay here with me. You're safe."

She closes her eyes again and turns her face away from my tender touch.

She doesn't say anything in reply.

"Talk to me," I urge.

"What do you want me to say?" That flat tone sets me on edge. It's far more disturbing than when she was screaming at me.

"I want you to say that you're all right. You know I'll always take care of you. Tell me, Abigail. Tell me you're mine." The last is rough with something like desperation.

Her next breath shudders as she inhales, but that's the only sound she makes.

"Answer me," I command.

"I've never been less safe in my life."

Her whispered words are a dagger to my heart.

"No," I refute. "I will always protect you. Always."

I've killed for her. I would do anything to keep her happy and safe.

Her eyes remain closed, her expression completely blank.

"There's no one here to protect me from you."

I reel back as though she's sucker punched me.

"You can't mean that." It's an order. I won't tolerate it.

I can't bear it.

"What do you want me to say, Dane? Just tell me what you want to hear, what you want me to do.

You've made it crystal clear that my wishes don't matter. You won."

I bare my teeth like a cornered animal, but she doesn't open her eyes to see my anguished expression.

"This was never a battle of wills," I correct her. "I don't want to *win*. I just want you. All of you."

"And you have me right where you want me. You made sure of that."

She doesn't even sound spiteful. That detached tone makes my insides churn.

"Not like this," I insist.

She has to look at me. She has to come back to me. Because even though she's right beside me, we've never been farther apart.

"I'm sorry I'm a disappointment to you." Another tear rolls down her cheek.

"You could never disappoint me. You're everything to me. You're all that matters. Abigail!"

She flinches and hugs her arms over her bare chest, shivering despite the heat of the bath.

"Two days ago, that would've been everything I wanted to hear," she admits quietly. "You can't possibly understand how horrific those words are now. You are incapable of understanding."

"Then explain it to me," I insist.

Or am I begging?

"I've already explained it, and you didn't want to listen. Instead, you chose to violate me again. You forcibly subdued me to shut me up and make me a compliant, obedient little pet. That's what you wanted, isn't it?"

"No." The word is almost a groan. "That's not what I want."

"Well, that's what you got. That's all I have left. It's all I can offer you."

"Abigail..." I choke on her name.

I open my mouth to try again, but a sound deeper in the manor puts me on high alert. Someone is here.

Have the staff returned despite my bribes?

"Daniel! I know you're here. Come out and face me."

My chest tightens.

No.

My brother can't be here. He can't see her.

Especially not like this.

Not like I've...broken her.

The prospect makes me dizzy with nausea.

"Stay here, little dove. I'll handle this."

I don't want to leave her alone right now, but she can't be part of this confrontation. She's in a delicate enough state as it is. She doesn't need to witness a shouting match with my little brother. Or worse.

The last time I saw him, it came to blows.

He was just a kid, and still, he tried to take me on.

That was his mistake. I don't possess the capacity for mercy, not even when it comes to my own flesh and blood.

Especially not when it comes to them.

I straighten and force myself to walk away from her. She doesn't protest or make a single sound of complaint when I leave.

She's probably glad to be rid of me.

Pain knifes through my chest, and for a moment, I think there might be something medically wrong with me. I've never felt this before. Surely, it's a sign of some terrible malady.

But I'm in excellent health.

A heart attack isn't at all likely.

I rub the center of my chest, straighten my shoulders, and stride out to face my brother.

He's standing in the corridor, waiting for me. I suppose it's a small mercy that he didn't barge into my bedroom. It's his house, after all. I surrendered my claim over it when I gave up my title and everything that went along with it.

"What do you want, James?" I demand, less coolly composed than usual.

The terrible confrontation with Abigail in the bath has shaken me to my core.

He eyes me up and down, then lets out a low whistle. "What the fuck happened to you? America not treating you well these days? Is that why you've come home? You look like shit."

"And you look like the same spoiled, arrogant little twat I left behind fifteen years ago."

He was only thirteen years old then, but he has the same dark auburn hair and eyes that match mine. A short beard covers his jaw now, but I still see a boy when I look at him.

His lips curl in a sneer. "Charming, as ever. Is this how you tempted your mystery woman to come to England with you? You must've truly swept her off her feet with your silver tongue. Or is it the family name you're trying to impress her with? You must've brought her to the estate for a reason. What's the problem? Is she not impressed with your massive...ego?"

The way he lingers over the insult makes it very clear that it's a slight against my manhood.

He knows about Abigail. That's far more worrying than his barbed comments.

"Who told you about Abigail?" I bark.

I don't want him to know anything about her, much less the fact that I brought her here against her will.

You kidnapped me, Dane. You drugged me and brought me to another country. Her accusation rakes through my thoughts, shredding me even as I attempt to gather my outward composure.

James' green eyes are wary on mine now. "You're different, big brother. I've never seen you worked up like this. America has changed you. Or is it her? Abigail, is it?"

"Keep her name out of your fucking mouth."

He takes a quick step back, then shrugs and returns to his nonchalant, spoiled prince posture. "Fine. Keep her secret. I really don't care. I only came to see if you were really here. I could hardly believe it when the groundskeeper told me this morning that you'd paid him to leave. Too bad you can't buy loyalty. You're not the heir anymore, Daniel."

"Yes, that's the whole point," I remind him coldly.

I didn't want to be the fucking heir. I refused to perform for them, to fit into the neat, small little box my parents designed for me. The cage they built with money and a "proud" lineage.

"But you're back," James counters. "Why?"

I hear Abigail moving around the bathroom: soft clatters of scented soap and the spray of warm water.

"Tea?" I ask blandly, gesturing in the direction of the grand staircase. "We can talk in the kitchen."

"I thought you'd never ask. I assumed you'd forgotten your manners."

Tea is always appropriate in England, even when verbally sparring with one of my oldest enemies. We can be civilized while utterly eviscerating one another.

12

ABIGAIL

I make quick work of washing the rest of the paint from my body, but by the time I'm clean and wearing a fresh dress, Dane is gone.

Someone else is in the manor. I heard them call out for Dane before he left me alone in the bathroom.

Or *Daniel,* as they had addressed him.

An old friend? Or a family member?

My first instinct is to scream for help, but no one is in sight.

Are they still here? Surely, they couldn't have left the estate already?

I recall the blood on Dane's face when he found me in the powder blue house, after he "talked to" Ron.

I will always protect you. Always.

If he thought that this unexpected intruder was a threat to me—or to his ownership of me—there's no telling what he might've done to them.

I force in a breath and try to get my brain back online in the wake of his devastating assault in the studio.

The assault that made me come harder than ever before.

Even when he was the masked man, my forbidden pleasure hadn't been so ruthless. Dane's sway over my body is like a hurricane: a destructive but awe-inspiring force of nature.

I shake my head to clear it.

I can't think about that right now. All I have room for in my brain is formulating an escape plan. This might be my only opportunity to get away from the monster who's holding me captive.

I tiptoe out into the portrait-lined corridor and find it empty.

I can't hear so much as murmuring voices in the distance.

Where is he?

If Dane catches me...

My heart hammers in my throat, and I swallow

hard against rising panic. There's no time for terror to take hold.

I break into a light jog, making my way toward the grand staircase as quickly and as quietly as possible. When I reach the top of the stairs, I'm met with more silence.

Dane and the anonymous visitor could be anywhere on the estate now. This house is so sprawling that I haven't even begun to explore the extent of it. And there's no guarantee that he's inside.

If I venture into the open, he might see me.

My descent down the stairs is shaky. Somehow, I will my knees to support me, and I make it into the cavernous entry hall. Sunlight pours through the huge windows that frame the front door on either side. And through the windows, the countryside sprawls on for miles. And...

I clap my hand over my mouth to smother my gasp.

There's a Jeep parked in front of the manor. I don't see a silhouette through the passenger window; the vehicle seems empty.

Whoever came to see Dane drove here in this Jeep. And for now, they're both mercifully out of sight and earshot.

Keys. I need keys.

My frantic gaze rakes over my opulent surroundings, and I can scarcely believe my eyes when they catch on a shining silver car key. It's been tossed carelessly on a priceless antique table beside the front door.

For a terrified moment, I eye the key like it's a viper that might strike if I reach for it.

Is this some insane test? Another mindfuck from Dane?

I shake my head and lunge for the key.

It doesn't matter. I have to try, even if it is an awful ruse.

The metal bites into my palm as I clench my fist tightly. I won't let go of this key unless Dane pries it from my fingers.

I throw open the front door, choosing speed over silence. My bare feet crunch across jagged gravel, but I barely feel the pain. I'm at the Jeep in seconds, and I fling open the driver's side door. I climb into the seat and jam the key into the ignition. The engine roars to life.

I barely take the time to sling on my seatbelt before I throw the Jeep in gear and hit the gas. The tires spin in the gravel, and then the vehicle surges forward.

"Abigail!" I hear Dane's roar even over the

revving engine, and I cast a fearful glance at the rearview mirror.

He's sprinting out of the house, chasing after me on foot.

As though he could possibly catch me now.

A giddy, mad laugh bubbles through the Jeep, and I increase my speed. Then I see the huge, iron gates ahead. They're closing. He's trying to lock me in.

He wants to keep me caged.

Not fucking happening.

The gates are only bracketed by a short brick wall that doesn't even extend fifty yards on one side. To the left is open countryside. This Jeep is more than capable of navigating the gently rolling hills.

I spin the wheel to the left, racing toward freedom.

My exhilarated laugh morphs into a sharp, short scream when the landscape drops out from under me. I'm airborne for a terrifying instant, and then the hood of the jeep tips downward. Bright green grass fills my view through the windscreen.

Metal crunches, the car horn blares, and pain explodes through my skull before everything goes black.

13

DANE

"Abigail!" I roar her name when the Jeep jerks sharply to the left, away from the closing gates. "NO!"

She doesn't know that the beautiful landscaping has been cut into a blind fence. The feature keeps troublesome sheep out of the estate while providing an uninterrupted view of the countryside. Instead of an unsightly fence, there's sharp a ten-foot drop that's unnoticeable if you don't know to look for it.

And she's racing right toward it.

My feet pound the curated lawn, and my heart hammers against my ribcage. I'll never reach her in time. There's nothing I can do to stop her. My stubborn Abigail is about to crash the Jeep, and I can't prevent it from happening. I can't save her. I can't protect her.

The disaster seems to happen in slow motion, each horrific moment imprinting on my brain to create nightmares that will last a lifetime. The Jeep is airborne for a split second.

Then comes the crash. The screeching metal. The blaring car horn.

I know what I'll find when I reach the wreck.

Blood. Death.

I'm as powerless as I was on that terrible night when I was five years old. Another crash, when I was a helpless child.

The sound that tears from my chest is something between a bellow of rage and a wail of anguish.

I can't lose Abigail.

I won't.

I refuse to live without her.

I swallow the copper tang of fear that coats my tongue and sprint toward the wreck. Whatever I find at the base of the blind fence, I'll have to face it head-on. If Abigail survived, she'll need medical care. She'll need *me.*

I can't allow old memories of long-buried trauma to rise up and consume me. I have to remain grounded in the present.

I have to save her.

She's alive. She's alive. She's alive.

I'm not sure if it's a prayer or an irrefutable truth that I'm willing into the world.

I finally reach the blind fence, and acid burns my throat at the sight of the wrecked Jeep. I curse my feckless brother for his carelessness in leaving his keys where she could easily find them. And for his foolish taste in vintage vehicles that lack modern safety features like airbags. A sensible car would've protected her from the worst of the damage, but this aged behemoth could've crushed her delicate body.

I leap off the blind fence and barely feel the pain that shudders up my left leg as my ankle twists. I manage to stumble toward her. I can see her lovely face in profile. It's covered in blood, and she's slumped over the steering wheel. Her eyes are closed. She's not moving.

Adrenaline increases my strength, lending me the leverage I need to wrench open the door. It screeches in protest, but I manage to get to her.

"Abigail. Abigail. Abigail..." I'm saying her name over and over, but she's not responding.

Her blood is hot and slick on my hand when I gingerly cup her cheek. My stomach turns in pure revulsion at the gory sight, but I force myself to study her wounds with clinical precision. She's bleeding heavily from a gash at her hairline. I can't tell how serious the damage is, but it's enough to have knocked her unconscious.

"Open your eyes, Abigail," I command. "Look at me."

But she doesn't obey.

The longer she remains unconscious, the higher the likelihood of brain damage. She could have a fractured skull. Internal bleeding.

All I can assess now is the fact that she fucking bleeding all over my hands, and she's as limp as a ragdoll.

I struggle to breathe through the fear that smothers my thoughts.

There's a pulse at her throat. She's breathing.

She's alive.

And she's going to be fine. I'll make sure of it.

"Dane?" James calls down to me. "Oh, fuck."

As much as I loathe him in this moment, my voice is rough with desperation when I beg, "Help me."

WITH JAMES' help, I'm able to get Abigail out of the wrecked Jeep and into another vehicle. I keep her gathered in my arms, murmuring reassurances to her as he drives the short distance from the base of the blind fence to the road.

We're in the back of one of my father's sleek black SUVs. If Abigail had chosen this for her insane escape attempt instead of the Jeep, she'd probably only have a few scratches.

Her escape attempt.

The thought makes my blood run cold. She was so desperate to get away from me that she risked her life. She'd begged me to let her go, but I'd selfishly refused because I didn't want to live without her.

Now that she might be bleeding out in my arms, I'm struck by the sudden, powerful realization that I *can't* live without her.

Abigail has given my life meaning. I won't tolerate a world without her in it.

I won't be able to endure it.

My vision blurs strangely, and I blink quickly to clear the burn from the corners of my eyes.

"Are you listening to me?" James demands. "The nearest hospital is almost twenty minutes away."

"She needs medical attention," I growl.

I'll do anything to save her, even if that means

walking into a hospital and confessing my crimes against her.

"You're a fucking doctor," James shoots back. "We have first aid facilities at the house."

My mind races. The faster I get Abigail medical care, the better. I'm one of the best surgeons of my age. I'll care for her with far greater attention than she'll get at hospital.

Because our survival depends on her recovery.

~

ABIGAIL HAS a deep cut on her forehead, but it won't scar, thanks to my neat stitches. The damage seems to be a flesh wound rather than a cranial fracture. Seeing her covered in blood had made me irrational, but now that she's stitched up and resting, I'm somewhat more composed.

She has bruised ribs and whiplash from the seatbelt cutting into her torso.

She'll be in pain for a while, but she'll live.

She will be okay.

And I will spend every day of the rest of my life making this up to her.

She stirs on my bed with a low groan, and I give her hand a gentle squeeze.

"You're safe, Abigail."

I'm right here, I want to add, but I swallow the reassurance.

When I'd washed the paint off her face, she'd said that she needed someone to protect her from me. My presence isn't a comfort to her.

But still, I can't let her go.

I know now that she's utterly essential to me; I can scarcely breathe at just the thought of losing her.

I rake my free hand through my hair. I've never felt so lost, so helpless. I don't know how to fix things between us. I can heal her body, but I fear I've done deeper, irreparable damage to her. To us.

"You're in love with her." James' quiet observation hits me like a blow to the gut.

I round on him with a glower. He doesn't understand the first thing about me. No one in my family has ever understood.

I'm not capable of love.

Obsession, yes. Possessiveness, definitely.

And above all, selfishness.

My absolute devotion to Abigail will have to be enough for her, because love is something I can never offer.

James holds up his hands in a show of surrender. "Fine. It's none of my business. I'll leave her in your capable hands now. And don't worry. I'm not going to run to mum and dad to tell them you're here. Let her recover fully before you go anywhere. I don't owe you anything, brother, but she doesn't deserve to be pulled into our family drama."

I narrow my eyes at him, usure if I should believe this show of goodwill. "And you're not curious about why she was driving away from me?"

He shrugs. "Like I said: none of my business. You're an arsehole. I'm not surprised you did something to make her pissed enough to leave you. But, Daniel." He pierces me with a dark green stare. "You can't keep her forever if she doesn't want to stay."

"You're absolutely right," I snarl. "My relationship with Abigail is none of your fucking business."

He sighs. "Arsehole."

I turn my attention back to my sleeping princess and barely register his retreating footsteps. For the foreseeable future, I'll have Abigail all to myself. I'll take care of her in her recovery. I'll prove to her that she can trust me.

She will love me again.

She has to.

14

ABIGAIL

The enormous weight of my failure makes my chest ache.

Or maybe that's the bruised ribs.

I barely managed to sleep through the night due to the fact that my entire body feels battered.

And the anxiety of sharing a bedroom with my assailant made me afraid to close my eyes. Even if Dane slept on a cramped, antique chaise that's far too small for him and doesn't look remotely comfortable.

When he stirred a few minutes ago, I closed my eyes and feigned sleep until he disappeared into the bathroom. I scarcely dared to breathe until I heard the shower running, and I knew that I was mercifully free of his presence for a short time.

I'm not ready for another confrontation. I'm not sure what he plans to do with me now that I tried to run away from him.

He'll probably find some other unfathomably sadistic way to make me suffer for daring to defy him.

I'm alone with him again on this vast estate. I have vague memories of another man hovering around my bedside yesterday. A man who closely resembled Dane, other than his auburn hair. They share the same striking, deep green eyes.

His brother was here.

And now, he's gone.

Did Dane hurt him? Did he make him disappear?

I shudder at the thought and suppress a wince at the answering flare of pain in my chest.

Surely, Dane's not capable of harming a member of his own family, even if they are estranged.

The latch on the bathroom door clicks, and I quickly close my eyes again.

"Abigail." He's using his disarming, bedside manner voice again. It's horrifically tempting to find comfort in it. "I need you to open your eyes. You hit your head hard enough to black out. I'll have to run some cognitive tests for a few days."

"I'm fine," I insist.

I don't want to interact with him at all if I can avoid it.

I hear him inhale deeply, as though he's struggling to maintain his calm demeanor.

"I need you to cooperate. Please." The last word is short and sharp, as though he's unfamiliar with the shape of it on his tongue.

I finally open my eyes and meet his gaze with defiance. "No commands this morning?" I ask bitterly. "What new mindfuck game do I have to endure now?"

His eyes flash with green fire, but his face remains impassive. "This isn't a game. You're injured. I'm going to take care of you."

"If I was hurt so badly, why am I not in a hospital?" I challenge.

He's too selfishly possessive even to take me for emergency medical care.

"It was too far away, and I ascertained that I'm capable of treating you here."

I glower at him. "At least be honest with me. You're too scared that if you take me to a hospital, I'll tell someone what you've done to me. You'll go to jail, and you don't want to risk that."

A shadow flickers at his jaw. "No one will care for you like I do."

I scoff. "Is that what you're telling yourself to justify this? I could've died, Dane. And you wouldn't have—"

"I know you could've died!" he thunders.

I cringe back into my pillows. I've never seen him so...feral. He's more unpredictable than ever, and fear prickles down my spine.

His entire body stiffens, as though he's willing himself not to move a muscle. I note that he hasn't approached the bed; he's maintaining several feet of distance between us.

Because he thinks he might hurt me? How tenuous is his control over his anger?

"Do you know how I..." He trails off and rakes a hand through his hair in a gesture of frustration I've rarely seen. "I can't lose you, Abigail."

"You mean you won't let me go," I counter acerbically.

He shakes his head, but it's not a denial. He looks almost weary. "I can't."

That's the only answer he offers me before he finally steps toward me. I flinch away. A scowl tugs at his handsome features, but he quickly smooths it away to a more clinical, calm expression.

"I'm going to do some tests now." It's a declaration, not a request.

So, we're back to subtle commands. He might try to pretend he's a good, compassionate man, but it's far too late for me to believe that carefully curated lie. He'll never ask me for anything; he'll simply tell me what to do. He expects mindless obedience, a pretty pet.

The pounding in my head is becoming too acute for me to argue further. Dane is a doctor, and there's no one else here to help me. After the crash, it would be stupid to deny medical treatment.

There will be time for defiance later. I won't try to physically attack him again, but I can go back to my original plan: make him grow bored of me.

I allow him to carry out the cognitive tests, and he seems satisfied with my responses.

"Where's your brother?" I dare to ask once he's finished.

His lips twist with distaste, but there's not so much as a flicker of guilt in his eyes. Either he's deeply psychopathic, or he didn't hurt his own kin.

With Dane, it's difficult to judge the situation. He's made it abundantly clear that he's a psychopath. What I'm unsure of is the depth of his condition. At times, he does seem to mean it when he's tender with me.

But that could be another part of his elaborate ruse, his sick mind games.

"James is back at his lodge in Wensleydale," Dane replies coolly. "He won't bother us again."

My brows lift. Maybe Dane isn't the only crazy one in the family.

"And he didn't care that you're holding me captive?"

The tiniest hint at a frown ghosts around his mouth, but he quickly catches it and returns to his calm demeanor.

"I didn't give him the details of our arrangement. He knows that you're mine, and he knows that you were badly hurt. We're safe to stay here until you fully recover."

"And then what?" I press. "What happens once I recover?"

He fixes me with a level stare. "That's up to you."

I press my lips together. I know he doesn't mean that I'll have the option to leave. He thinks he'll break me in the time it takes me to get better, and then I'll meekly follow wherever he leads.

"What do you plan to do to me in the meantime?" I challenge.

I won't give him a reason to assault me again, but that doesn't mean he won't expect sex.

"I plan to take care of you," he grits out. "You have nothing to fear from me. I'll prove it to you. Let me."

I huff out an incredulous breath. Is he really commanding me to trust him?

I don't bother to tell him that's not how trust works.

"I scared you yesterday," he says quietly. "I understand that now. You weren't ready, and I pushed you anyway. I didn't know how being together like that would upset you."

"You think I like it," I fling his sickening words back at him. "I don't."

His jaw tightens. "Now's not the time for this conversation. I don't want to argue. You need to rest and recover."

I bristle at the fact that he's essentially telling me to shut up again, but I swallow more defiant words.

He's right. I do need to recover. I can't get out of this nightmare if I'm injured.

"I'll get you something to eat," he says. "Food, then painkillers. I don't want to see you suffering."

Again, it's all about what he wants. Not the fact that I'm in pain. He's incapable of true empathy.

I close my eyes again, shutting him out in the only way that I can. He doesn't make a sound for several long seconds, but finally, I hear him stomp out of the bedroom.

I know my reprieve will be short; he'll come back with breakfast in a few minutes. Without his infuriating presence to draw my ire, pain consumes me.

~

AFTER BREAKFAST, the painkillers finally start to take effect. I ease back into the pillows, cushioned in fluffy clouds. The absence of pain is almost euphoric, and some part of me registers that I'm probably a little high from the strength of the drugs he gave me.

But I'll take the dulled awareness over the pounding in my head and sharp stabs at my ribs with every shallow breath.

"Screen time is inadvisable," Dane says. "I'll read to you so you don't get bored."

I blink and manage to focus on him. He's sitting on the too-small, pale blue chaise, his massive body almost comically oversized for the delicate antique.

I instantly recognize the book he's holding, even though his big hand conceals most of the title.

The Invisible Life of Addie LaRue.

My favorite book. The one we bonded over.

I choose the dark god too. His remembered words torment me. At the time, they'd been a revelation, a miracle. The man I wanted so desperately understood my desires. It'd seemed like a dream, too impossible to be real.

I should've trusted my instincts.

"What made you pick up *Addie LaRue*?" I ask, even though I'm reluctant to hear the answer. "You never did tell me."

He cuts his eyes away. "I think you know."

Yes, some part of me did already know. He's broken into my apartment. He must've seen the book at the top of my stack.

Uncomfortable silence stretches between us. I don't have to reply or ask more questions.

He's my stalker, my attacker.

And yet, when he starts reading my favorite book aloud in that deep, rumbling voice, I sink into the familiar story.

It's so much easier than facing the horrors of my reality.

"You'll want a bath. You'll have to be careful with your stitches, but you can get properly cleaned up."

My stomach turns. "I have no interest in getting naked with you."

His nostrils flare with irritation. "I didn't ask you to get naked with me."

"No, you didn't ask at all. Do you even know how to make a request? How to ask for my consent?"

He sighs. "I'm tired of arguing. It doesn't have to be so contentious between us."

I lift my brows at him but don't say anything in response. I will not make life easy for him.

"I don't intend to bathe you, as much as I would like to." At least he's honest enough to make the admission, even if he is making a concession for once. "You need to rest and recover. I'm not going to cause you distress."

"Of course," I say dully. "This is about making sure your pet recovers."

He sighs again, a more exasperated exhalation. "I do want you to recover, Abigail. Is that so terrible?"

"Depending on your reasoning, yes. It can be."

"My only desire is to see you healthy and whole. Your pain is unbearable to me."

I eye him with suspicion. It almost sounds as though he truly cares.

But I can't trust a word that leaves his sensual lips.

I am in pain, and I do want a bath. After the crash yesterday, I was too woozy take care of myself, and Dane was merciful enough not to bathe me.

"It's been over twenty-four hours since you hit your head," he says, the reasonable doctor. "I'll need to monitor you closely for the next few days, but you're well enough to see to your own essential needs. However." That one word fills me with dread. "I don't intend to leave you completely on your own. You're still a fall risk."

I eye him warily. "What are you planning to do to me?"

Something like pain tightens his features. Have I managed to wound him?

"I'm going to help you walk to the bathroom," he explains, soft and placating. "Nothing more."

I grit my teeth and accept his help getting to my feet. After a brief dizzy spell, I'm able to walk the few steps to the ensuite. He hovers at my side, allowing me a modicum of personal space while remaining close enough to catch me if I stumble.

It's almost as though he's keeping a respectful distance.

I don't know how to process that, and my head hurts too much to puzzle it out.

When I enter the bathroom, he doesn't leave, but he does turn his back.

"I'll be right here if you need me." He says it like a reassurance.

And maybe it is. I don't want to be with him, but he's not forcing himself on me. He's remaining nearby in case I get dizzy again.

I can't succumb to his tender care. It's rooted in selfishness, not true concern for me. If he really cared, he would take me to a hospital. He would walk away and never show his face again.

But I know that won't happen.

So, I strip and carefully step into the bathtub, which is already filled with warm water. Dane set it up for me.

He doesn't care, I remind myself.

I can't forget his true nature for one second.

Even when he retrieves the worn copy of *Addie LaRue* where it was waiting on the sink and begins to read to me.

It's not my own copy—I've memorized every crack in the spine of my beloved book.

That means Dane's the one who's worn down the book in his hands. It was brand new when he brought it into the café, I'm sure of it. I clearly remember the perfect condition when I first saw it tucked in his hand.

How many times has he read it since then?

It's another puzzle that I can't bear to contemplate for long.

He's not the only one who's tired of arguing.

I relax into the warm water and allow my mind to drift as his voice fills the room in a cultured, soothing cadence.

15

ABIGAIL

The studio is the only place in the manor where Dane leaves me alone. Over the last three weeks, it's become my personal haven.

Otherwise, he's a constant presence—he cooks every meal for me, cleans up after us, and reads to me for hours. We've moved on from *Addie LaRue* to one of my favorite fantasy romance trilogies. He doesn't seem to mind the romantic content, and the steamy scenes read aloud in his deep voice makes something flutter between my legs despite my best efforts.

He hasn't tried to touch me more than absolutely necessary in that time, and he's slept on the tiny chaise every night. He says he doesn't want to disturb my sleep, but sometimes I wonder if he has other reasons for giving me space.

My plan from the very beginning was to make him understand that I will never love him again. Perhaps my escape attempt—and the desperate risk I took—has given him some perspective. It might actually be sinking in that I don't feel anything for him but loathing and resentment.

I can see that it bothers him.

Good.

He deserves to feel disturbed for what he's done to me.

I'm not delusional enough to think he experiences guilt, but he does seem uncomfortable and off-balance around me in a way I never would've expected.

I've spent long days in the studio working through my physical pain so that I can spend time at my easel.

Dr. Graham approves of my efforts to return to gentle daily activities as part of my recovery, even if he does appear genuinely bothered by my winces at sudden movements. A few times, he's reached for me during particularly intense spikes of pain, but he always withdraws when I flinch.

Today, I'm putting the finishing touches on the

painting I've struggled to express on my canvas. The agony of it was far deeper than the ache in my ribs when I lifted my arm or shifted my weight too quickly.

I set my brush down and sit back, taking in my work. It hasn't been a cathartic project; it's been an act of anguish.

But it's finished. I can show it to Dane now.

I cross the parquet floor and open the door to the portrait-lined corridor.

"Dane?" I call out.

Heavy footfalls immediately rush toward me. He appears out of his bedroom and storms down the corridor. His dark brows are drawn together, and his eyes are almost feverish with worry.

"What's wrong?"

I take a step back from his potent aura. I don't understand him when he's like this, and it scares me. I can't predict his actions when he shows a semblance of human emotion. Will he tackle me to the floor again and force himself on me in a moment of twisted passion? Or will he snap back to his cold, clinical default state? Both are equally terrifying.

I swallow hard, and he halts as though he's hit a brick wall, stopping several feet away from me. His beautiful eyes rake over my body, assessing me for signs of injury. Then his shoulders slump slightly.

"You're all right."

"I have something to show you," I say instead of responding.

I'm not all right. My heart throbs as though it's as battered and bruised as my body after the crash. The painstaking work of finishing my painting has left me wrung out and emotionally exhausted, but I have to see this through.

I take another step back, but this time, I'm welcoming him to enter the studio. The moment he sets eyes on my art, he freezes again.

"Abigail…" He breathes my name. "What is this?"

"It's me," I answer quietly.

On the canvas, I've captured all of my pain and impotent rage, my fear and desperation. My face is contorted in an anguished scream, and blood drips from my split lips. My face is bruised almost beyond recognition, and my fingers are knotted in my hair, tearing at the delicate strands. More bruises encircle my throat—the violent marks from Dane's fingers imprinted on my pale skin.

"Why?" he asks, his gaze transfixed on the disturbing image like it's a car crash he can't look away from.

"This is what you did to me." It's meant to be a flat statement of fact, but the lump in my throat makes the words strained.

"No," he refuses. "You're getting better. You're healing. This didn't happen in the wreck."

"It's how I feel inside." Tears burn my cheeks. I blink rapidly, but I can't stop the steady stream as my tumultuous emotions leak out of me.

He shakes his head sharply, a willful rejection of the truth. "I know men have hurt you," he growls. "I know you've felt shame and self-loathing. I never want you to think of yourself this way."

"No, Dane. This is what *you* did to me."

He rounds on me, and I can't help cringing away. His entire body coils tight, and I'm not sure if he's preparing to launch himself at me or if he's wresting with his own shadows of emotion. The only ones he's capable of experiencing.

"I would never hurt you," he vows. "Never."

"You have hurt me more deeply than anyone in my life. Worse than Tom when he raped me. Worse than my family with their years of psychological and emotional abuse. You made me believe I loved you, but it was all a manipulation to get me into your bed. It was all a sick game to you." I dash the tears from my cheeks so I can look him squarely in the eye. "You broke my heart, Dane. You broke *me.*"

His skin is unusually pale, and he looks like he might vomit. "I wouldn't. I haven't."

"Look at me." I gesture at the painting. "Look at what you've done to me, and tell me you would never hurt me. Tell me you truly believe that you haven't shattered me. Lie to us both if you want, but I'm done being gaslighted by you."

He stares at the painting again and shakes his head. Then he stares some more. The silence is thick between us, and I let him stew in it.

I'd expected to feel vindication in this moment, but all I feel is soul-deep grief.

Grief for what I thought we could be together, and for the devastating loss of love when I learned the truth about Dane.

"I wanted to die," he rasps.

"What?" I ask faintly.

He finally turns to face me, and his eyes are dark with agony. "When you crashed the Jeep, I thought..." He swallows hard. "All that blood. You weren't moving. You didn't answer me when I said your name."

His jaw firms, and he fixes me with a fiery stare

that's so intense I can hardly bear to maintain eye contact.

"If you had died, I would've opened my veins and laid down right next to you. I realized that truth in the moment I thought I'd lost you."

Shock punches me when he drops to his knees and takes my chilled hands in both of his. My fingers are trembling, but not from fear.

"I told you I can't live without you. I mean it in the truest sense of the words. You've made me *feel* for the first time in my life. I wasn't living before I met you. My life has no meaning without you in it."

My lips are parted on panting breaths, as though I've been sprinting for miles rather than standing frozen in the beautiful studio that he made for me.

"I know I've hurt you. I can see that now. I will spend every day of the rest of my life making it up to you. Name anything you want, and I'll give it to you. I'll give you the world, Abigail. I would give you the blood from my veins. I would give you my heart, but I can't promise you something I don't have. You want the organ that keeps me alive? I'll cut it out of my chest for you. Because without you, I don't need it."

He rubs his thumbs over my chilled knuckles. "I'm scaring you. I don't want to, but I won't lie to you. I'm obsessive and cruel and every bit as selfish as I've ever said. I won't ask you to forgive me. I can at least spare you that selfish request." He lifts my hands and kisses my palms with reverence. "I'll be better for you, Abigail. I will never be worthy of you, but I'll be better. I swear."

His pain pierces my heart like a knife, twisting and shredding. Even after everything he's done to me, bearing witness to his anguish is my own form of agony.

I want him to be the man I fell in love with so badly.

And this version of Dane who's on his knees before me looks so much like him.

I know deep in my bones that this isn't a trick. It's not another manipulation.

He said he would die without me, and I believe him.

I don't know how to process it.

I hate him for what he's done to me, but how can I still feel yearning for the man who assaulted me?

The depth of his obsession is terrifying. His confession should only make me more wary of him, but my tattered heart tugs toward his in an echo of the love I used to feel.

"I don't know what to say," I finally admit on a shaky whisper.

He grasps my hands closer to his chest. "You don't have to say anything. You don't owe me anything. I'm the one who should speak now. And I want to say I'm sorry. I'm so fucking sorry I hurt you like this. Never again. I swear."

I'm stunned at his apology. It seems impossible, surreal, that Dane is on his knees telling me he's sorry. I didn't think he was capable of remorse.

But he's still not promising to let me go if that's what I ask of him. He said he won't live without me. That means I have no hope of escape.

My heart breaks all over again.

I'm still trapped with the madman who wears my love's face. And his devotion to me is more fanatical than I ever could've imagined.

He'll keep me in this gilded cage forever, and I fear that one day, I may no longer want to fly away.

He reaches up and brushes the tears from my cheeks with his thumbs.

"I don't want to make you cry."

Now I'm the one sinking to my knees. They're too shaky to support me. My chest convulses on a harsh sob.

I want him, and I hate myself for it. No one has ever cared about me the way Dane does. It's tempting and terrifying in equal measure.

His arms close around me, strong enough to support me but gentle with my healing body. True to his word, he's not causing me an ounce of physical pain.

My tormented soul is another matter entirely.

"I've got you," he promises.

"I know." I choke on another sob. "I know."

16

DANE

Blood. So much blood. It's splattered across my face in droplets that are beginning to cool. It's wet and sticky on my hands where I'm grasping my sister's dress. I'm shaking her, screaming at her.

Katie isn't breathing. She doesn't answer when I say her name over and over again.

How can she answer when half her face is missing?

A car horn blares incessantly, deafening me. I shake my head sharply, as though I can toss the maddening sound from my ears.

I can't escape from it. My seatbelt is stuck.

If it weren't, I would've tumbled into my sister.

The Jeep is on its side. We rolled off the country lane

and down a steep hill when my father took a particularly fast corner.

I don't know how long we've been here, but it's dark outside, and my voice is raw from screaming.

No one has come to save us.

No one has come to save Katie.

My father is slumped over the steering wheel. It's not an unfamiliar sight to see him passed out after a night of drinking, but this time, there's a thick crimson stream that flows down his slack face.

The car horn rings in my ears. I'm clawing at them, raking my hands through my hair as though I can pull the sound from my mind.

Katie is looking at me with one eye, but she doesn't see me. She doesn't see anything.

I cry out for help, for salvation, for mercy.

Anything to escape this nightmare.

After a while, I go quiet. I accept that no one will come for me.

No one will bring my twin sister back to me.

I don't yet know a word for what's happened to her, but I know she's gone forever.

The doctor won't be able to fix her.

There's nothing I can do. I'm powerless. Helpless.

Alone.

"Dane." A soft hand shakes my shoulder.

I grab the delicate wrist and force the tender touch away.

Abigail reels back into the shadows of my bedroom. I shove upright off the cramped chaise and blink hard to focus on the present.

I run a hand over my face and find that my brow is slick with sweat.

"I'm sorry," I murmur into my palm. "I didn't mean to lash out at you."

I'm not ready to face Abigail. Not when she'll look at me with fear in her aqua eyes.

"You were having a nightmare," she says gently.

The bedside lamp turns on, chasing the shadows away. I keep my face in my hand and apply pressure to my closed eyes, as though I can wipe the macabre images from my mind.

"You're shaking," she observes, voice soft.

I rub my temples and keep my eyes closed. "I'm fine. Like you said. It was just a bad dream. Go back to sleep. I'm sorry I woke you."

"Who's Katie?"

I freeze. No one has said my sister's name aloud since her funeral. Certainly not in this house.

She deserves better than that. She deserves to be remembered.

And I've spent years trying to forget.

I haven't thought about that crash in a long time, and nightmares about it haven't troubled me since I was a child. I never needed to be coddled or comforted when I was distressed in the middle of the night; I learned to overcome the fear on my own.

Comfort wouldn't have been forthcoming, anyway.

"My sister," I admit. "My twin."

"I didn't know you have a sister. You've never mentioned her."

"That's because she's dead." The words are flat and utterly devoid of emotion. "She died when she was five years old."

Her small gasp makes something twist in the center of my chest.

"I'm so sorry." She sounds like she really means it. My sweet, compassionate Abigail. "You were having a nightmare about her? You said her name in your sleep."

I press my lips together for a moment, reticent to reveal the terrible extent of it. My father's carelessness. My mother's coldness. The fact that they replaced my dead sister with James and acted as though she never existed.

But Abigail doesn't have an ounce of cruelty in

her. She won't dismiss Katie's memory as an inconvenience.

I can trust my little dove.

"I was dreaming about the night she died," I say after a long, heavy pause.

"You were there?" Abigail's voice is soft with horror. "When you were only five?"

I nod absently, detaching myself from the volatility of that night and looking at the memory with cool, clinical eyes.

It can't hurt me if I don't relive it.

"My father was driving drunk. A bad habit of his. He thinks he doesn't have to follow the law when it's inconvenient to him. He was driving us through the Dales when he took a corner too sharply. The Jeep rolled a few times. My father was unconscious for several hours. Katie didn't make it."

"Dane..."

My name wavers, and I finally look up at Abigail to find that her remarkable eyes are shining with tears.

Tears for my sister.

For my loss.

My chest aches, and it's all I can do not to reach for her when I know she'll recoil again.

"Is that why you..." She trails off and then tries

again. "When I crashed the Jeep. I understand why that must've been so upsetting for you. I didn't know."

I try to shrug, but it's a sharp movement to throw off her empathy. I can't allow her emotions to bring out the new feelings she evokes in me.

Not when it comes to this.

Because if I feel what I felt that night, it'll destroy me.

Maybe it already has.

Then, by some miracle, she's closing the distance between us. She sinks down onto the chaise beside me and places a tentative hand on my knee.

I can't help grasping it and pressing her palm directly over my aching heart. She doesn't pull away.

"When I saw you covered in blood..." My breath shudders. "I wasn't rational. I was consumed by the fear of losing you. If James hadn't snapped me the fuck out of it, I wouldn't have been able to help you. I'm sorry."

"You did help me," she says with the weight of a promise. "You healed me and took care of me. You are taking care of me. I'm right here, Dane."

She places her other hand on my cheek, and I forget how to breathe.

"What you went through is terrible. No one should endure that."

"I couldn't save her," I confess. "I didn't know how to fix her."

"You were a child." Her thumb caresses my cheekbone, keeping me grounded to her. "Is that why you became a doctor? So you can fix people?"

I try to scoff. "I've told you before that there's nothing altruistic about my career."

"But you could, if you wanted to," she counters quietly. "You have the knowledge to save someone if they're seriously injured. You saved me."

I wish that were true. I want to be the man she's describing, but it's just not who I am.

"You were never in danger of dying. I just patched you up."

"But you didn't know that when you first found me in the Jeep. You said there was a lot of blood. I was unconscious. I know that must've been traumatic for you." She increases the pressure of her hand over my heart. "I'm safe now, Dane. You can breathe."

Bright, hot hope sparks in my chest.

She said she's safe with me.

Before, she'd said that she needed protecting from me.

Has something changed her mind?

I scour my recent memories to understand this change in her. Maybe my unnervingly intense apology hadn't frightened her like I thought. Yesterday afternoon—after she showed me her nightmarish self-portrait—I'd thought she'd been distressed. I overwhelmed her and made her break down sobbing.

No. That can't be what's changed her mind, no matter how sincere my apology was.

It must be this: the fact that I've told her my worst trauma.

I've made myself vulnerable with her.

The power she holds over me should be terrifying, but I want her too badly to care. She's looking at me with that clear, open gaze for the first time since I brought her to England. She *sees* me in a way no one else ever has. No one has ever bothered to try.

I obey her gentle urging and draw in a deep breath. Calm settles over me, and my eyes droop closed with a sudden wash of exhaustion.

Her hand turns in mine, pulling away from my chest. My fingers tighten around hers, but she's not trying to escape me; she's urging me to follow.

"You should sleep in the bed," she says. "That chaise can't be comfortable."

I look at her with wonder. Is she offering me absolution? Or at least acceptance?

I scarcely dare to hope.

"I don't want you to pity me."

"This isn't pity," she assures me and climbs into bed, making room for me beside her.

I join her before she can change her mind. She scoots back slightly, and I get the message: I can sleep beside her, but she still wants space.

I can give her that.

For now.

I'll win her back, no matter how vulnerable I have to make myself. Nothing matters but having her.

"My father likes to drink too," she says after we settle down, inches apart. "And he doesn't care who he hurts when he's drunk. Usually, it's verbal cruelty. But it still hurts." She places her delicate hand over mine again, the lightest contact. "I'm sorry for your loss. I'm sorry about Katie."

Just the sound of someone else saying her name in this house, acknowledging her existence, is enough to make my eyes burn strangely.

"Thank you. I am too."

Another beat of silence passes before I growl,

"You said *usually*. Has your father ever laid a hand on you?"

"I don't think we should talk about this."

"Why not?"

She's looking at me with that clear-eyed gaze again, and it takes everything in me not to glance away from the power of her guileless stare.

"Because I don't know what you might do to him if I tell you."

That answer is enough to seal his fate, but she won't want to hear that.

"I'm serious, Dane." She reads me so easily. "You can't hurt my father."

I decide to bargain with her. "I won't, if you tell me what he did."

She considers me for a long moment, assessing my honesty. Whatever she sees in my expression, she must decide that she believes me.

"It hasn't happened since I was about ten," she begins. "But he used to belt me if I disappointed him. Or angered him. He got angry a lot when he was drinking. At some point, I guess he decided I was too old to discipline me like that anymore. The cruelty was verbal after that. He would yell, and then my mother would dictate the terms of my punishments."

"And what did she do to *punish* you?" I can't quite keep the dangerous edge from the question.

"You can't hurt my mother either."

I growl, then catch myself. "Fine. I won't hurt anyone in your family. No matter how much they deserve to suffer."

"Swear it."

I narrow my eyes at her. I don't want to agree to this blanket pardon of her loathsome relatives.

But she would be troubled by their suffering. She's so soft-hearted and good to her core. She would shed tears even for her abusers, just like she said she cried over her rapist's death.

I won't allow the monsters who raised her to cause her one more shred of grief. And she would grieve them if I killed them for her. She would probably feel responsible.

I won't do that to her.

"I swear I won't hurt anyone in your family."

She nods, accepting my promise.

"My mother's punishments were erratic," she admits. "Sometimes, I wouldn't be allowed to leave the house for a week. Other times, a simple slap to the face was enough to satisfy her. There was no rational pattern to the severity of the consequences."

"The chaos was designed to keep you on edge."

Her mother is a narcissistic piece of shit. I'd known as much after spending five minutes in her presence at Meadows' wedding.

But learning the extent of her cruelty to my Abigail is enough to make me see red.

"Dane." My name is laced with warning, and I realize my hand has fisted beneath hers.

I force my muscles to relax.

"I'm not in that house anymore," she reminds me. "She can't hurt me."

"And you'll never step foot inside it again." I try to keep the ring of command from my tone, but I don't quite succeed.

"I don't intend to."

"I'll protect you from them," I vow. "I'll make sure they never bother you again."

"You can't guarantee that," she counters, but she doesn't seem troubled by my fierce countenance. "I can handle them."

I remember the way she wilted like a cut flower in her mother's presence at the wedding.

"You don't have to handle them alone. Not anymore."

She stares at me for a while, and I realize she's not going to respond to my intense declaration.

"We should get some sleep," she says instead.

"I'll be here if you have another nightmare and want to talk."

I marvel at how she's softened toward me.

Maybe she won't hate me forever.

Maybe she'll love me again one day.

17

ABIGAIL

I*'m safe now, Dane.*

I can hardly believe I said those words to him last night. They'd been automatic, an irrepressible urge to comfort him in the wake of his nightmare about losing his sister.

But had I meant it?

Yesterday, he confessed that he would die without me. The man who fell to his knees and literally offered me his heart wouldn't hurt me. He wouldn't be capable of it.

Nothing will erase the pain he's caused me. Nothing can undo the stalking and kidnapping. The lies and the heartbreak.

But I don't think he'll hurt me again.

When he first brought me to England, I railed at

him that he was tormenting me, that he was my own personal monster. He hadn't listened. Convincing him that he'd wronged me seemed impossible.

Now, he's apologized. He acknowledged that he caused me immense pain. And it was so much more than a simple *I'm sorry.*

I'll be better for you, Abigail. I will never be worthy of you, but I'll be better. I swear.

And last night, he was so raw. He told me how he watched his twin sister die because of his father's carelessness. He welcomed my comforting touch, as though he needed to feel me.

I thought he was a complete psychopath. But he does seem to feel something for me. Maybe it's every bit as cruelly possessive and obsessive as he claimed. That doesn't change the fact that my ravaged heart feels tethered to his by a gossamer thread.

We both have emotional wounds inflicted by our families. It was one of the first things that bonded me to him.

That had nothing to do with his stalking, nothing to do with the thrilling fear I experienced around him—the fizzy sensation I'd mistaken for lust.

This part of our connection has always been real: we've both been subject to abuse.

It made me kind, but it made him cold.

I never want to hurt anyone the way my parents hurt me. But Dane seems to have shut off his feelings entirely to avoid the pain.

He was only five years old when he watched his sister die. I can't imagine the psychological damage that inflicts on a child.

"What are you thinking about?" Dane's eyeing me almost warily.

I realize I've fallen a few steps behind him, and I've been staring at him like I can peer into his mind if I just look hard enough.

I cut my gaze away and study the stunning landscape. We're walking along a vaguely marked footpath through an idyllic field dotted with sheep.

Dr. Graham has deemed that I'm well enough for light exercise, and I jumped at the chance to explore the countryside. For weeks, the views from the manor's windows have been tempting me to paint the rolling hills, but I was too focused on my anguished self-portrait.

"Can we talk more about last night?" I ask after a moment.

He pauses, then leans back against a dry-stone wall. His posture is casual, but there's a defensiveness in his crossed arms.

"What do you want to know?"

I know this topic will be painful for him, but I have to understand him better. And not just so that I can formulate an escape plan. I'm starting to accept that I simply long to know everything about him.

Some secret part of me wants to justify opening my heart to him.

I'm nowhere near loving him again, but I do feel compassion for him.

And yearning for the man who knelt before me and promised to give me the world. All he wants is me. The knowledge is heady and terribly tempting. I've been alone for so long, and Dane promises complete and utter devotion.

I consider my next question carefully. I could ask why he decided to assault me as the masked man again, but I fear that his answers will be the same as before. He thinks it was the best way to win my heart.

That subject is too painful to contemplate, so instead, I ask, "What were your parents like with you? After Katie died?"

His brow furrows. "Why would you ask me that?"

"I told you how my family treated me when I was a child. Is it too much to ask for the same in return?"

He manages a halfhearted smile. "Do you promise not to kill them if I tell you?"

It's not funny, but I return his smile, my lips twisting with sorrow for the abused child he used to be.

"I promise," I vow needlessly. His family is in no danger from me, no matter how awful they are. I hope to never meet them.

"They didn't beat me, if that's what you're asking," he says, tone light.

"That is what I'm asking," I confirm. "So, what did they do to you, Dane?"

His eyes focus on something beyond me. "It was the opposite of what you experienced. Your father belted you, and your mother punished you. They controlled you with physical and verbal violence."

"What's the opposite of that?" I press.

"Complete indifference. Duty and expectation. Raising me like I was nothing more than an extension of their own vanity. Everything for appearances, nothing real. Nothing raw."

"No emotions," I surmise.

He sneers. "What good are emotions if there's no one there to bear witness to them? Why bother with the theatrics when you're alone? Why suffer through them when they're of no consequence?"

My heart bleeds for him. For years, I've felt so alone.

His damage matches mine, even if it shaped him differently.

Suddenly, he pushes away from the wall and closes the distance between us. He takes my hands in his, but he doesn't force me closer.

"You *see* me, Abigail. Ever since the night we first met. You make me feel things I never thought possible. No one has ever given me that gift. I don't think anyone else can. There's only you. You're all that matters to me."

Longing floods my chest in a surging wave that's strong enough to make my healed ribs ache. My head tips back, and for the first time in weeks, I allow myself to truly breathe in his salt-kissed cedarwood scent. Comfort blankets me, even as my body heats in response to the scent memory.

Before the terrible night I stepped into the powder blue house, this was all I wanted: Dane's arms enfolding me, keeping me safe and giving me more pleasure than I imagined possible.

I still want that. I still want him.

Not the monster who kidnapped me.

Not even the man I thought I loved back in Charleston.

But *this* man: the real Dane.

Nothing about him is a lie. He's raw and vulnerable. He can't live without me.

"What are you thinking?" he asks me again. He's staring at me so intently that I shiver like his gaze is a palpable caress on my soul.

"I don't want to think anymore."

It's foolish, reckless. But I cup his beautiful face in both hands and draw him toward me for a fierce kiss. I don't stop to consider what this means. What the consequences may be.

I melt into him, wrapping my arms around his shoulders to pull him even closer.

He meets me with the hungry growl that makes my insides quiver with fear-edged delight. His sensual lips are so decadently soft on mine, worshipping the shape of my mouth. Tasting me with teasing flicks of his tongue, testing my welcome.

I open for him on a sigh, completely surrendering to my desire for him.

His tongue surges into my mouth, claiming me in deep, domineering strokes. I'm dizzy from his kiss, the passion we share.

How could any woman give this up? How can I walk away from such perfect chemistry?

He no longer allows me room to resist, and I

don't want to. His arms are iron around me, immovable but cradling my body with care. One hand grasps my nape in a firm grip, holding me in place so he can ravage my mouth.

My fingers spear into his thick, midnight hair, and I drag him to me, urging him to take me more deeply. I share every breath with him, and my heart races for him.

Rain begins to fall, and I welcome the cooling mist on our heated skin. It dampens his hair, and the thick, short waves tighten into loose curls. I twine them around my fingers, reveling in the feel of him against me.

It feels like a cruel eternity has passed since our last kiss. I'm a different woman than I was then. This is a different life.

One that I'm sharing with him, whether it's by my own choice or by his will.

In this moment, I choose to be with him. To stop twisting myself in knots and just let go.

And it feels so blissful that my eyes sting with the force of my emotional release. I close them and kiss him like I need him more than oxygen.

The rain is falling in fat, cool drops, and I shiver despite the heat between us.

Dane breaks the kiss, fixing me with a cocky smirk at the sound of my small whimper of protest.

"Let's get out of the rain. Come on."

"I don't mind," I insist, wanting to stay in this surreal, peaceful bubble with him for a while longer. "It's at least half an hour to walk back to the house. We're wet anyway."

"There's shelter nearby. The rain will pass soon, and then we can walk back." He grasps my hand and starts walking. "No more arguing, Abigail."

I huff out a breath, but I don't really feel annoyed. I'm still burning for him, and I remember the pleasure I used to experience when I obeyed his every wicked command.

"I don't like it when you tell me to shut up," I inform him.

He quickens our pace as the rain falls faster. "I would never tell you to shut up. I love the sound of your voice too much. I simply don't want to argue."

I love the sound of his voice too. That gorgeous, lilting accent when he caresses my name with his tongue. The way his tone deepens when we're intimate. The way he rumbles when he reads my favorite books to me, like rolling thunder during a warm summer storm.

We arrive at a tumbledown stone building that

used to be some sort of barn or small enclosure for sheep. Now, half of the roof has fallen in, and it obviously hasn't been functional in many years.

"It's safe," Dane reassures me as we duck under the remaining shelter. "I've been coming here since I was a boy, and it hasn't changed one bit."

"Your home is so beautiful," I say with fervent sincerity. This estate has some of the most stunning landscapes I've ever seen. I can hardly wait to paint them.

He chuckles. "We're standing in a ruin during a downpour. It's soggy and gloomy. I'd hardly consider that beautiful."

"You're just not looking properly," I tease. "Don't you see the way the sunlight plays over the hills?"

He steps toward me, and for a moment, I think he's going to kiss me again. His face is sharp with hunger, and I tip my head back to welcome his claim.

Instead, his big hands bracket my waist, and he spins me so that I'm facing away from him, looking out at the landscape. He pins me to his front with his firm grip on my hips.

His breath warms my rain-chilled neck as he murmurs in my ear, "Tell me more. Describe it to me."

I'm compelled to respond. Not by his commands, but because I hear the yearning that roughens his voice. He wants to see what I see.

I lean back into his strong body, and just like on our first dates, the world comes into sharper focus. The countryside is naturally verdant, but now the color palette turns almost surreal.

I point down the length of the valley. "The river looks so blue at this distance, like a shiny, navy satin ribbon that some careless goddess has dropped between the hills. And the way the afternoon light hits the lake makes it glitter with gold sparks." My gesture shifts to the rolling hills. "It's gloomy here, but farther away, you can see the shadows of the incoming rainclouds dappling the grass. How many shades of green do you think I would need to paint to capture it? I'm not even sure if I can."

"You can," he says with the weight of an oath. "You are remarkable, Abigail." He nuzzles my hair and twines my purple curl around one elegant finger. "I've never seen the world the way you do. You make it brighter and more beautiful than I ever thought possible."

"Dane..."

The way he talks about me is overwhelming, like

I'm his own personal miracle. He believes in my art. He understands me like no one else.

He applies steady pressure to my curl, tugging gently until I turn my face to his. He captures my lips again, and I don't hold anything back. I pour all of my tumultuous emotions into the kiss: my longing, my pain, my turmoil. And above all, desire. It's carnal and desperate, hot enough to sear away reason and self-doubt.

I don't break the kiss as I turn into him, pressing my chest to his. My nipples are hard, aching peaks against the inside of my bra, and I wantonly arch into him to seek stimulation. His hand snakes under my cotton shirt, and he palms my breasts with a squeeze that takes me to the edge of pain. Molten honey pools low in my belly, and my core pulses for him.

His cock presses into my thigh, hard and insistent.

But he doesn't try to force himself on me. He doesn't take anything more than what I'm offering.

He seems to read my moment of worry, because he breaks the kiss to promise, "Tell me to stop, and I'll stop. No need for a safe word. This isn't a game. I need your consent. I can't hurt you again."

He says it roughly, like the thought alone threatens to break something in him.

The belief that he won't hurt me settles in my heart and takes root. He truly means it.

And my body is still thrumming for him.

"Yes," I pant against his lush mouth. "Yes, I want this. I want you, Dane."

His low groan rumbles into my chest when he captures me in another fierce kiss. My fingers fumble at his belt, and his free hand is shoving at my jeans. He finds my hard clit and rubs in a firm rhythm that I like best. At the same time, he tweaks my nipple in a cruel pinch.

A sizzling line of fire races straight from the abused bud to my stimulated clit, and I hit my peak with shocking speed. The orgasm crashes through me, and I claw at his jeans as my fingers curl with the force of my pleasure.

I start to come down from my quick high, but we're not nearly finished. He tears at my clothes, stripping off the sodden garments until I'm naked for him. My flesh pebbles in the slight chill, but I grab his hand and drag him out from under the sheltered part of the barn. We're still in the stone walled enclosure, but the rain falls down on us in fat, heavy drops. The cool dichotomy with my desire-heated skin makes every inch of my body hypersensitive.

He barks out a delighted laugh and joins me in the deluge, stripping off his shirt and baring his chiseled chest. Rain runs down his rippling muscles in enticing rivulets, and I grab him closer so I can trace one with my tongue.

He bites out a curse, and I smile against his hard chest.

I can make this fierce man come undone. I make can make him laugh. I can make him *feel.*

I'm giddy with the knowledge, the power I hold over him. He could subdue me in a moment, but he won't. Not without my consent.

I'm safe here, in this wild, gorgeous landscape with the most beautiful man I've ever known.

He frees his cock from his jeans and grabs my waist, yanking me into him. Then he lifts me up, and I wrap my legs around him for support, clinging on tightly. My shocked laugh mirrors his, a sound of release and merciful joy after long weeks of pain and anguish.

He backs me up against the aged wall. The stones are slick and rough against my back, but his big hands cushion my ass and shoulders. He won't let me get so much as a scrape while we're together.

His cock presses at my entrance. I'm wet and ready for him after the ruthless orgasm he wrung from my body.

He pauses, brow furrowing. "I don't have a condom."

"I trust you," I promise.

That's a worry for later. Right now, I need him inside me more than I need my next breath.

With my vow of trust, he enters me in one swift thrust. I cry out at the shocking penetration, and he stills, fingers flexing into my skin.

"I'm okay," I assure him. "It's good. So good. Don't stop."

We're a perfect fit, his huge cock stretching me just to the edge of pain with his deepest thrusts. I remember the first time we had sex, when he'd made sure I was relaxed and ready to accommodate him. He'd been ruthless with my body back then, too, but he'd ensured my pleasure. So much pleasure that I'd wept for mercy.

I shudder at the bittersweet memories. The man fucking me with such passion now is the same person. The way he's holding me, sheltering me, is the same. I didn't fully know Dane back then, but this hasn't changed.

Our chemistry is as potent as ever.

With each harsh thrust, pleasure builds at my core. My fingernails dig into his shoulders, and he releases a primal snarl. His teeth nip my lower lip in punishment, but I claw him harder.

"Abigail!" I think it's meant to be a warning, but it comes out as a feral roar.

The sound of Dane coming undone for me pushes me to the peak. Rain splatters my upturned face as I scream out my release. He fucks me harder, his lips pulling back from his teeth like a beast as he resists his own orgasm so that I can reach completion.

When he can't take it anymore, he pulls out, and hot cum lashes my belly and thighs. The rain immediately begins to sluice it away, erasing his mark. The loss draws a soft cry from my chest.

He cups my cheek and studies my face like I'm his greatest treasure. "Are you all right?"

"Yes," I promise, placing my hand atop his to anchor him to me. "You didn't hurt me."

And now, I'm sure that he never will.

18

DANE

Two Weeks Later

I can hardly believe that Abigail willingly sleeps in my bed and welcomes me into her body every night. Only a few weeks ago, that seemed like an impossibility. After the crash—when she'd tried so desperately to get away from me—I'd been determined to keep her. But I hadn't been sure if she would give herself to me ever again.

My sweet, compassionate Abigail still wants me. It wasn't my mastery of her body that made her surrender; it was my vulnerability. Raw honesty.

I'll answer any question she asks of me if it

means more intimacy with the woman who is my everything.

Her birth control shot should be effective by now, so I won't have to use the precaution of condoms anymore. The feeling of her wet cunt gripping my cock when I claimed her in the rain was the most exquisite ecstasy of my life.

She didn't ask where I obtained the shot, and I chose not to tell her about the delivery. I think we're both avoiding difficult topics.

Like the fact that I won't allow her to leave me. I won't risk her running to a driver to ask them for rescue.

She seems completely absorbed in her work, shutting herself away in her studio for hours every day. It wasn't difficult to get the shot delivered while she was painting. I have the necessary professional documentation to obtain what I wanted. The arrangement was easy enough.

And it'll be well worth it when I get to fuck her without the barrier of a condom separating us.

We haven't engaged in anything more than slightly rough sex since that day in the rain, but I know she needs more. I worry that she's not ready to accept the darker things we both enjoy, but I can tell she's not fully satisfied. I've seen Abigail when she's utterly spent and sated, and I'm determined to make her that blissful again.

I have a plan in place to coax her darkness back to the surface, but that will have to wait for tomorrow.

No matter what happens, I will not force her again. She'll get her safe word back, and I will honor it.

I'll do anything to keep her trust.

"Dane?"

I'm rushing toward her studio without hesitation. She doesn't sound distressed, but I can't help feeling on edge whenever she's out of my sight. After the crash...

I shake off the bloody memories and focus on her sunny smile.

"I'm fine," she promises, reading the worry that lingers around my brow. "I want to show you something."

She steps back, inviting me into her private haven.

For a moment, I falter. The last time she showed me something in her studio, it was her horrific self-portrait. That confrontation had shredded me. These last two weeks together have been so wonderfully easy. I don't want to go through another difficult conversation like that.

"Don't worry," she soothes. "It's nothing bad. Well, I hope you think they're good. I've been working really hard, and I'm feeling so inspired. But they're nothing special. I like them, though. What do you think?"

She steps back, revealing three small impressionist paintings. One is still on the easel, and the other two are propped against the wall on either side of it.

"Abigail," I breathe.

"I know they're not masterpieces or anything," she rushes to downplay her art. "But it's just so beautiful here, and I wanted to try to capture it. They're silly. I don't plan to frame them or anything like that. They're just for me. But I wanted to show you."

"Abigail." Her name is a quiet interruption this time. She's babbling because she's anxious about my reaction, but I'm speechless.

I stare at the paintings, and something tugs at the center of my chest.

The one against the wall to the left of the easel is the view through our conservatory—probably her first glimpse at the Yorkshire Dales from the kitchen.

The painting to the right is a close-up of a grey

stone wall. She's captured the dull sheen from the rain, and a broad, masculine hand is splayed against the wall. Thick veins stand out on the back of the hand, and the fingertips curve as though clawing at the stone for purchase.

It's my hand. When I braced myself after fucking her against the wall in the ruined barn.

The third painting holds my attention the longest. It's the scene from the barn, the one she so eloquently described with her artist's eye. But the perspective is slightly different. The rolling, sun-dappled hills are the same, as is the blue river and the glittering lake.

It's the two figures in the foreground that fascinate me. Their backs are to the viewer, but a tall man with dark hair is embracing a smaller woman. She's barely visible—the only hint that she's there is the perfect purple curl that's twined around his finger.

They look like they belong there.

Like it's home.

"What's wrong?" she asks. "Did I not get it right?"

I shake my head, struggling for words.

"That's not me," I finally manage, pointing at the man in the central painting.

"What?" She peers at her work with a critical

eye. “There’s something off about your hand. I know. I worked at it for days, but it’s just not—”

“Your art is perfect,” I assure her. “But I’m not... This isn’t my home. I don’t want it to be.”

Her lips part, and her eyes shine for a moment before she blinks quickly. “I didn’t mean to upset you. I’ll put these away.”

Fuck. I’m saying all the wrong things when she was making herself vulnerable by sharing her work with me.

“Your paintings are masterpieces, and I intend to frame each of them,” I say sternly.

If I have my way, she’ll be featured in a gallery soon. But she’s not ready to accept that yet.

“This place is messing with my head,” I admit. “I chose to walk away from my title and everything that comes with it, including the estate. I hated this place when I was growing up. But you see it so differently than I do.” I gesture at the painting again. “I don’t belong here.”

Her features are pinched with concern. “It doesn’t have to be your home if you don’t want it to be. You can choose your home. I chose mine. Back in Charleston.”

She cuts her gaze away, and for a moment, I

think we're going to return to the thorny issue of her leaving Yorkshire. Without me.

"This place holds nothing for me but memories of cruelty and blood," I say before she can go down that road.

Her eyes snap back to mine, bright and incisive. "You're talking about your sister's death? The car crash?"

I run a hand through my hair, and now I'm the one to look away. "Yes."

"But it's more than that." She sees right through me. "You can talk to me, Dane."

I don't want to tell her some of my darkest truths, but I have to prevent her from thinking about Charleston.

"I was a violent child," I admit. "I was the cruel one. Well, we all were, I suppose. Except maybe James. He's just a spoiled little prince." I force myself to meet her eyes. "My parents are cold and narcissistic, but they never beat me. My mother always said she didn't know where I got it from, and I guess that doesn't really matter. The fact is that I was dangerous. It wasn't until I was eleven that I realized I had to hide that part of myself."

"Dangerous, how?" she asks carefully.

"I lashed out at other children. I hurt them."

All those times I came back with little spots of their blood dotting my shirts, and my mother would berate me for ruining my pristine clothes. Not because we couldn't afford more, and not because she cared about the other children. She only cared about what other people would think if they found out.

At least, the people who *matter.*

If the children of staff members had "accidents" around the estate, my parents didn't give a fuck. And if their parents put up a fuss, hefty bonuses made the problem go away. Or outright dismissal if my mother was irked enough.

"What changed when you were eleven?" Abigail presses gently. "Why did you stop being violent?"

"I almost killed another child. A child who *mattered*, according to my mother."

I force myself to continue over her horrified gasp. I'm staring at the painting of us together, the one that looks so right but all wrong at the same time.

"Peter was a bully," I explain. "He often picked on me for being a freak. The other children were right to sense something off in me. I wasn't good at concealing it back then. I didn't even try.

"I never retaliated at school because I knew better than to get caught. But then one day, Peter was tired of never getting a reaction from me. So, he ran his mouth about Katie. He said I'd probably killed my sister. He said it was my fault she was dead." I glare at the painting. "I shoved him out of the window. He spent two weeks in hospital."

Abigail doesn't seem to have the words to respond to that cold declaration, so I carry on.

"The police were called. I was questioned. Mum made it very clear that I would be locked up if I didn't figure out how to mask my true nature. She said I was lucky that Peter's family accepted a payoff and a few threats with the weight of the family name behind them." I sneer around the last. "She thinks she can buy anything she wants. People. Freedom. Absolution."

I stop talking. I've said too much.

Abigail is far too quiet, and I don't dare to look at her and see her expression of revulsion.

"You were a traumatized child." Her softly spoken words hit me like a blow to the chest. "It sounds like you didn't have any support after you saw your sister die. Your father was responsible for her death, and he didn't suffer any consequences, did he? That's what you mean when you say your mother thinks she can buy anything. Isn't it?"

I stare at her with open awe. "You're not... You

don't think I'm a monster for what I did to that boy? I hurt people, Abigail. Children."

"You were a child yourself. You had witnessed something horrible, and you were living in an emotionally abusive home. It doesn't sound like anyone showed you another way to behave, and you lashed out."

"That doesn't scare you?" I challenge, hardly able to believe she's not cringing away from me.

"There have been plenty of times when you've scared me, Dane. Now isn't one of them. I'm not afraid of the boy who suffered so much pain. I'm sorry you went through that."

I just told her I almost killed a child, and she's apologizing to me.

She truly is my miracle.

I decide not to say anything else that might change the way she's looking at me right now: like I'm worthy of compassion. Empathy. Affection.

"I didn't know you felt that way about the estate," she says. "I can change the painting. I can destroy it if you want me to. We can burn it together."

I grasp her hands in mine, pulling her close. "No. Never destroy anything you create. Especially not on my account. The world needs your art."

Her cheeks color my favorite shade of pink. "I'm really not that talented."

"Yes, you are." I look at the central painting again, the one of us standing together, looking out at the countryside. "You made a place I loathe look like home. That's a gift, Abigail. Don't you dare hide it or destroy it."

The longer I look at the painting, the more it feels right. And I start to realize that maybe it's not the setting that makes it feel like home. Maybe it's that perfect purple curl curved around my finger.

19

ABIGAIL

"Where are we going?" I ask warily.

Dane has been enigmatic about our destination, and his teasing non-answers are starting to grate on me.

"Back to Charleston?" I ask, but I don't sound as hopeful as I should.

I tell myself that's because it's highly unlikely, not because some part of me doesn't want to leave this peaceful space I've found with him. As long as I don't think too hard about going home, I'm able to indulge my growing, irrational desire to stay with him, despite everything he's done.

"Do we look like we're dressed for travel?" he drawls, shooting me an unbearably sexy smirk from the driver's seat of the sleek black Porsche.

I huff an exasperated breath, and he chuckles.

He's wearing a sharply tailored tux, and he's dressed me in a daring silk gown. The neckline drops down almost to my navel in a deep V, and he's chosen a gorgeous purple tone that's so dark it's almost black. I didn't argue when he gave me the obviously expensive garment. We're past that now.

I'm so tired of arguing with him, and I believe him when he says that his gifts don't come with strings attached. After his intense revelations about his abusive family and his choice to walk away from them, I know he would never try to control me like that.

And he'd wanted to hurt my parents for their controlling behavior. I'd had to make him promise not to go after them if I revealed the depth of their cruelty.

This isn't about controlling you. It never has been. I want to take care of you.

I didn't understand him when he made that fierce declaration, but I know him better now. I *see* him: the devoted lover and the fierce protector. And I see the pain that shaped him into a selfish psychopath who learned to turn off his emotions entirely in order to protect himself.

That side of him doesn't scare me anymore.

"We're almost there," he promises.

"Almost where?" I demand, irritated and more than a little nervous. Anxiety tightens my stomach, and a familiar, giddy thrill races through me at the hint of fear.

"You'll see."

"Dane."

"Abigail."

I throw up my hands and ignore the way that stern, deep tone makes my core heat.

We've been driving through the countryside on a narrow, winding road for nearly an hour, and the sun is setting.

The headlights turn on, illuminating a twilight-dim turn onto an even narrower driveway. We pass through open iron gates.

Is this another family estate?

After a further five-minute drive, we slow behind a line of other cars. Ahead, the vehicles curve around a circular driveway in front of a grand, sprawling house that almost rivals the Graham family manor.

My jaw drops.

He's going to take me somewhere public? Where I can ask someone for help?

I narrow my eyes at him. The arrogant bastard

must think I'm beyond that now. He must've decided that I don't want to escape from him.

I cross my arms over my chest.

Don't I?

I'm no longer sure if I do, but my heart longs to return home to Charleston. I can't stay in this surreal state with Dane forever. No matter how much I'm coming to care for him, I can't just abandon my life. I won't live to suit his every whim. If I choose to stay with him, that's not how it will be between us.

He's insisted that he wants *me* so many times. Not a mindless, obedient pet.

He hasn't even called me *pet* in weeks, not since I crashed the Jeep during my escape attempt.

I almost miss the kinky endearment.

I press my lips together to hold in further questions. I'm not sure what I want to say.

And I'm not sure what I'll do once I'm surrounded by people who can possibly help me get back home to Charleston.

Without Dane.

We come to a brief stop behind a yellow Lamborghini.

He takes the opportunity to turn toward me and grasps my hand. He lifts it to his lips and brushes a gentlemanly kiss over my knuckles. For a moment, he's my dashing, perfect prince again: the man I fell for all those weeks ago.

Then his wicked grin reminds me that he's a rakish villain too.

They're both the same man. Exactly how I used to fantasize about him when he was just a customer, an untouchable, beautiful god.

His thumb brushes my palm. "I trust you, Abigail. I trust in *us.*"

My heart skips a beat.

If I betray him now, he'll end up in prison. I'll never see him again.

The thought makes my stomach knot.

"You'll need this," he says, releasing my hand.

I instantly miss the reassuring warmth of his tender touch. My fingers furl and unfurl, as though grasping for him.

His attention is on something in the glove box, so he doesn't see my involuntary, embarrassing display of desperation.

Something glints in his hand: a golden masquerade mask.

His soft fingers brush my cheeks as he lifts it to my face, and his touch is so alluring that I don't try to pull away when he fixes my mask in place. It covers my features from my cheekbones to my brows. Someone who knows me well could probably recognize me, but a stranger won't be able to make out all of my features.

Dane puts on his own mask. Unlike mine, it's black, but it glints dully like carbonite. It only covers the upper half of his face as well, but it's been molded to subtly mirror the shape of a skull.

He looks like a beautiful demon, some sort of terrifying incubus that's designed to lure me in and ravage me.

My mind flashes back to a different night when he donned a skull mask. It'd been stark white, and it'd completely concealed his face.

I shiver, but I can't stop staring at him: my dark god.

"Are you frightened?" he asks, voice low and intimate.

"Yes." The affirmation shudders from my chest.

"Are you turned on?"

My cheeks heat, and I glance away, hiding from him. Hiding from the truth.

Two fingers curl beneath my chin, and he redirects my gaze to his. In the dim lighting, his eyes are almost black, enhancing his aura of otherworldly danger.

My heartbeat ticks up a notch, and I feel an answering pulse between my legs.

"What are we doing here?" I ask instead of answering his lewd question.

He traces the shape of my mouth with his thumb, and my lips tingle with sensual awareness.

"I'm going to remind you of how it should be between us. I'm going to give you what you really want."

"Dane..." His name is a protest. I can't bear it if he forces himself on me again.

"You have your safe word," he promises. "Use it, and everything will stop."

I shake my head, so he cups my cheeks to still the sign of my fearful denial.

"Tell me that what we've shared over the last two weeks has been enough for you," he challenges gently. "Tell me you don't want me to take control. You don't want me to ravage you."

My chest tightens. It's been blissful to be back in his arms, to have him inside me. But I haven't experienced the transcendent ecstasy that once consumed me.

But that was before I knew what he did to me. Before I knew how dangerous he truly is.

"I will never hurt you," he reminds me. "Trust me."

"Dane, I..." I can't find the right words. My mind sticks on the decision.

It's foolish to give in to this, to give in to *him*. He's my stalker. My kidnapper.

And yet, I know deep in my bones that he'll do anything to keep me safe. Even from himself.

He brushes another kiss over my knuckles. "It's your choice."

We've reached the front of the line of cars. He gets out, circles the Porsche, and opens my door for me. A valet takes his keys, and Dane places his hand at the small of my back.

Butterflies beat their delicate wings in my stomach, a slightly desperate, fearful thrill.

He pauses and snaps his fingers. "How could I forget?"

The slightly cruel tilt to his smile tells me that he didn't forget at all; this moment is designed to keep me on edge.

He reaches into his pocket and pulls out my black leather collar with rose gold accents. The one that used to mark me as his submissive. And he was my master.

I try to take a step back, but his strong arm snakes around my lower back, trapping me. He pulls me in close, and his murmured words are hot on my neck.

"Are you going to be a good girl and lift your hair for me? Or am I going to have to pin you down to lock your collar around your pretty throat? One way or another, you'll accept it. You'll accept *me*."

My lips part in shock, and I stare up into his glittering green eyes that peer through the black skull mask.

"It's your choice," he says again, but there's a mocking lilt to his tone this time.

I can't allow him to physically subdue me like that. I can't bear it. Especially not when there are other people around to witness my degradation.

My hands shake as I lift my hair, but I glare at him with open defiance.

He grins. "There's my fierce pet. You're being such a good girl for me now. When will you show your claws?"

"I'm not playing this game with you," I hiss.

I can't.

Not after what he's done to me. Not after that awful scene in my studio, when he forced orgasms from my unwilling body.

He drops a kiss on my chilled lips, and the ice that was beginning to frost my skin melts away.

His hands encircle my throat, and smooth leather touches my neck. The familiar feel of it buckling into place is bittersweet, and tumultuous emotions surge.

I can't do this. I can't want this.

But I don't fight when he slips the delicate padlock through the metal loop at the back of the buckle. It clicks closed, and the collar seems to meld into my skin, becoming part of me. As though it belongs there.

As though I belong to him.

I'm so absorbed by my internal conflict that I barely register the glint of silver before the cuff closes around my right wrist.

"What are you—"

The question dies in my throat when I see him lock the matching cuff around his left wrist. We're tethered together by a short chain.

"You're not going anywhere, pet."

I straighten my shoulders. "You can't do this to me. I won't walk into a room full of strangers wearing a collar and handcuffs."

"I absolutely can." He chuckles, a sound of arrogant amusement. "Try to stop me. Give me the satisfaction of clipping on your leash and making you crawl."

I narrow my eyes at him. "You can't make me do anything."

"Oh, little dove," he croons. "I definitely can. But for now, I'm giving you a choice."

"These aren't choices," I shoot back. "It's coercion."

With every "choice" I make, I'm making myself more vulnerable. I'm surrendering to him just a little bit more.

He traces the curve of my purple curl. "And you love being coerced."

You liked it. I remember how he justified his actions as the masked man. How he justified what he did to me in the studio.

The chill is closing in on me again, and my throat tightens to restrict my breathing, as though his long fingers are squeezing my neck.

He kisses me again, taking his time to caress my lips with his, imbuing me with warmth.

"Time to join the other guests, pet."

I try to stall, but he strides forward. The metal cuff tugs at my wrist, dragging me in his wake.

"This is crazy," I insist.

I'm wearing a collar and handcuffs. I can't be seen publicly like this.

He laughs again and doesn't slow his confident pace through the massive, open front doors. "Don't worry. You'll fit right in."

Dozens of people wearing fine clothes and elaborate masks fill the foyer. Several curious glances rake over us, witnessing the embarrassing spectacle we're making.

To my horror, I feel something slick between my thighs with every shaky step. I'm getting turned on by this humiliating scene.

I lift my chin and school my features to an impassive expression that's far better at concealing my emotions than the gold mask.

"My proud, brave little pet." Dane says it like praise, not mockery. "You'll enjoy yourself tonight. I guarantee it."

As we near the other guests, shock makes my feet stick to the marble floor.

The guests' outfits are obviously expensive, but several of them are dressed in leather and latex rather than fine silk. A statuesque blonde wears a corset over her voluminous taffeta skirt. Her breasts are almost spilling out, and the skirt is open at the front to reveal sheer white tights. She's not wearing underwear.

I gasp and tear my gaze away. It falls on the man to her left. What I originally thought was a formal kilt is actually crafted in leather, and his loose-fitting white shirt is unbuttoned to reveal masculine chest hair. He's holding a leash causally in one hand. The other end is clipped to a collar on the corseted woman's neck.

"What is this, Dane?" I ask breathlessly.

He fixes me with a wicked smirk. "It's a party, darling. Haven't you always wanted to go to a ball like one of your fantasy princesses?"

I gape at him. There's nothing romantic about this. It's deviant. Carnal.

Perverse.

And my blood is humming through my veins.

"That's one of my favorite colors," Dane rumbles, caressing my heated cheek. "Almost as pink as your pretty cunt."

"Dane!"

Judging by the kilted man's smirk, he heard that scandalous remark.

A server carrying a silver tray with Champagne flutes pauses to offer us a drink. Dane assesses me with an x-ray gaze, reading every nuance of my jittery, indignant mood.

He selects a glass for himself but doesn't offer me one.

"I'd rather not end up with Champagne in my eyes," he teases. "I have a feeling you'd toss the drink in my face as soon as it was in your hand."

"Good idea," I mutter.

"Sorry to disappoint you. Now, do you want a drink?"

I blink at him. He just said I couldn't have one.

"Yes," I reply before he can change his mind. Now that he's mentioned it, I would very much like to throw Champagne into his smug face.

One of his big hands slides into my hair at my nape, anchoring me in a firm grip. He applies steady pressure and tugs my head back slightly. He lifts the glass to my lips.

"You wouldn't," I insist.

He won't actually give me a drink from his hand like I truly am his helpless pet.

"Your choice," he says again, but he doesn't lower the glass.

I press my lips together in denial, but I can't shift my head. The glass tilts despite my glower, and

Champagne spills down my chin, dripping onto my chest.

I open my mouth, cheeks flaming. Having him pour the drink down my chest feels more embarrassing than accepting the drink. The fizzy liquid bubbles over my tongue, reminding me of the drink he bought for me on our first date.

That memory is so terribly tempting, and for a moment, I want to give in.

I want to belong to Dane again. In every way.

But the Champagne is still spilling from the corners of my lips, and I realize he's doing it intentionally.

"Not too much," he chides, as though I have a choice in how much I'm drinking. "I don't want your senses impaired."

I consider spitting the Champagne in his face, but it's too late for that. He pulls the glass away, and I'm left panting for breath and covered in expensive wine.

His eyes darken when they fix on my chest, and I realize my nipples have pebbled to hard, aching buds. They're clearly visible against the dark purple silk. It clings to my breasts now that the material is wet.

"I want a taste," Dane rumbles, but he sets the half-empty glass on to a passing server's tray.

I try to ease away from his predatory energy, but the handcuff keeps me closely bound to him. And he still hasn't released my hair.

He tugs sharply, forcing me to expose my throat. His lips are unbearably soft against my sensitive skin, and his tongue brands me when he licks the line of my vulnerable artery. He takes his time sampling the Champagne on my skin, making his way lower down my chest with a trail of hot, hungry kisses.

"No." My protest is so breathy that it might as well be a welcoming purr.

His lips close over my nipple, his teeth grazing it through the thin barrier of my wet dress. Pleasure floods my body in a strong wave that crashes from my breasts all the way to my fingers and toes. It goes straight to my head, and for a moment, I'm euphoric. Desire layers over my embarrassment, and sparks dance down my spine to heat my core.

"Lovely." The woman's voice is far too close.

Oh, god. I remember all of the people that surround us. They're all bearing witness to my shameful, wanton responses to Dane's cruel game.

I lift my free hand and try to shove his head away

from my chest. He bites my nipple in sharp reprimand.

I yelp, and the woman giggles.

I turn desperate eyes on her and suppress a whimper as Dane returns to teasing my tight, sensitive bud with his tongue.

"Help me," I beg. I can't bear further humiliation, no matter how my body is humming for him. "I don't want this."

Dane nips at me again, and my knees almost buckle. He steadies me with an arm around my waist and continues to torment my breasts as though this is completely normal and natural.

The blonde fixes me with an indulgent smile, and one blue eye winks through her silver mask. "Of course you don't."

"You don't understand," I insist, and the words are almost a desperate groan. "I don't want to be here."

The woman's smile tilts. She thinks this is a game.

And Dane is still tormenting my nipples in the way that makes me come undone for him.

"No," I moan, equal parts horror and lust. I try to keep the woman in focus when my eyes are threatening to roll back in my head. "I'm here against my will."

She giggles again and sips her Champagne, indulging in the carnal scene like a spectator at a particularly sensual play.

"He kidnapped me!" I burst out.

Someone has to help me. This has to stop.

But Dane doesn't stop. He drags his tongue up my sternum before his teeth graze my throat in warning.

"Please," I beg the woman. "This is real."

She just continues to smile at me. "I'll leave you two to enjoy yourselves."

"No! Wait!"

But she doesn't listen.

No one listens to me. No one will help me.

The cruelty of Dane's dark game crashes down on me, and I shriek out my frustration. Several people look at us, but they don't seem alarmed in the slightest. Instead, they're merely curious. Interested to see what Dane's *pet* will do next.

My right hand is cuffed to his left, and his free hand is still in my hair.

My left hand slaps his stunning face with a shocking *crack*.

I immediately regret it.

His wicked grin is far more terrifying than a thunderous scowl.

"Are you ready to struggle, little dove?"

"I want to leave," I insist, my chest rising and falling on rapid, heaving breaths.

"It's too late for that," he admonishes. "Do you really think I'll let you go unpunished?"

"Don't do this," I beg. "Not in front of all of these people."

His fingers soften in my hair, and he massages my scalp in soothing circles. "Is it the audience that bothers you so much?" he croons. "Beg, and I might show mercy."

I lick my lips, shame searing my cheeks. I don't want to beg him for anything, but I can't endure more of this erotic torment.

My pride makes my spine stiffen, but I force out through gritted teeth, "Please. I want to leave."

"You didn't ask very nicely, but you'll do better by the end of the night."

For a moment, I think he'll refuse. I think he's going to force me to remain here where everyone can witness my degradation.

Then he lifts me over his shoulder and strides out into the night.

I huff out a relieved breath, but I don't yet realize that this isn't over. It's barely even begun.

20

ABIGAIL

"Where are you taking me?" I demand.

"You asked to leave the party," he reminds me, like he's being completely reasonable.

"Take me back to the car."

"I never agreed to that." His low laugh is infuriating, and my inner muscles clench.

I cover my face with my free hand, relieved that he can't see my chagrin when I'm slung over his shoulder.

He's taking me somewhere deeper in the shadowy grounds of the grand estate. Night has fallen, but Yorkshire is far enough north that the sky is still dusky despite the late hour. I've seen enough to know that we're in a curated garden; I noted perfectly pruned rose bushes and a neat hedge in my peripheral vision. Otherwise, I'm looking down at the dirt path beneath Dane's designer shoes.

Too late, I realize that the hedge has risen up on either side of me. I've been so absorbed in my inner turmoil that I didn't pay enough attention to my surroundings.

We're in a hedge maze, and I'm already hopelessly lost.

Dane seems to know exactly where he's going.

"Put me down. I don't like this," I say shakily.

"Liar," he drawls.

His restraining hand eases up my thigh to caress my swollen pussy through my thin dress. I gasp at the answering burst of pleasure and buck over his shoulder. His only reply is another arrogant chuckle.

"Bastard," I hiss.

"I'll enjoy taming that pretty mouth later. I have other plans for you now."

He finally sets me down, and I'm disoriented for a moment at the shift in perspective. I blink and realize we're in the center of the maze. A bubbling fountain featuring giggling cherubs is illuminated to our right. The small statues seem to mock me with their sly smiles.

Dane bends down and rummages in a waiting black duffel bag.

"What's in there?" My voice is a touch higher than usual.

"You'll find out soon enough."

"You planned this," I accuse. "You've arranged all of this in advance."

He quirks a single dark brow at me. "Of course."

"You knew no one would help me."

His sensual smirk is pure, masculine satisfaction. "I have you right where I want you."

I lift my chin and glare at him. "You wouldn't put me in a scenario where you could get caught. I thought we were building trust, Dane."

"That's exactly why we're here," he explains calmly.

He's holding a short coil of rope in one hand. My stomach flips, and I try to edge away from him.

What else is he hiding in that bag?

"If you think I'm just going to stand here compliantly while you tie me up, you're mistaken," I defy him. "I won't let you."

He pins me with that wickedly sharp smile. "I'm counting on it."

His hand jerks to his side, and my cuffed wrist forces me close to him. Before I can reason through how I can deny his twisted game, he twists my arm behind my back and grabs the other. Rope loops around my wrists, binding them together at the small of my back.

"No!" I try to twist away.

Which is exactly what he wants. He wants me to struggle, to indulge in his dark mindfuck.

I know this, but I don't soften and submit.

I can't. My pride won't allow me to surrender so easily.

And some secret, perverted part of me doesn't want to remain meekly compliant.

The metal cuff unlocks, dropping to the dirt path. But my wrists are even more securely trapped than they were before.

I lunge forward, propelling myself away from him. He loops an arm around my waist and drags me back.

"No running yet. We're not finished here."

My heart hammers against my ribcage.

Yet.

He's going to chase me through this maze, and I have no idea how to get out.

I harden my resolve and try to elbow him in

the ribs. His sharp exhale is my only reward before I'm shoved to my knees. He grabs my shoulders and forces me down onto my back, trapping my hands under me. His weight settles over my hips, just heavy enough to pin me without causing me pain.

I writhe in the dirt, but when he fists my dress in both hands, I arch toward him. With one jerk of his powerful arms, the delicate material tears, baring my breasts to him. He cups them with reverence, teasing my nipples with his thumbs.

Pleasure sparks beneath his tender touch, and I swallow a whimper.

"No one else will ever see you like this. You're all mine, Abigail."

We're alone out here, completely isolated from the rest of the party. I don't have to worry about anyone witnessing my humiliation anymore.

"No one will save you from me," he warns, and I shudder.

He keeps me pinned and reaches into that damn bag again. Something jingles softly when he pulls it out. I instantly recognize the silvery glint of nipple clamps.

This isn't the first time I've seen them, but they're different from the ones he's used on me before.

These are connected by a black leather cord, and three delicate silver bells hang from it.

"Don't you dare."

"How else am I supposed to keep track of my pet when she runs away?" he taunts.

"I'm not your pet," I seethe, wriggling beneath him.

All I manage to do is stimulate my clit against his growing erection.

He hisses in a sharp breath as his own lust torments him, but he doesn't have an ounce of mercy in his hungry gaze. The light from the fountain catches in his eyes, illuminating the dark green pools so that they practically glow.

He's so unbearably beautiful: my dark god.

He hums in false consideration. "Aren't you? Pets wear pretty collars, just like yours." He leans in close, his lips teasing mine as he says, "Pets obey their master."

I snap my teeth at him, and his eyes flash with delight.

He grips my jaw, holding my head still so that I can't sink my teeth into his perfect mouth.

"No biting," he admonishes sternly. "I'll tame you again, Abigail. It will be my pleasure."

Wanton arousal wets my thighs, and my clit

pulses madly against his erection. It takes all my willpower to prevent myself from rubbing against him like a needy kitten.

He plucks at my nipples, drawing a reluctant moan from my chest. His deft fingers feel so decadent, tormenting the tight peaks with pain that blossoms into forbidden pleasure.

I throw my head back on a sharp cry when he captures them in the clamps. They bite down on my sensitive nipples, and I squirm in the dirt. I must be getting filthy, but he wants me this way: dirty and degraded. I never knew how the humiliation could make me burn for him.

He stares down into my eyes and twists the screws on the clamps, adjusting them until they're tiny vises on my throbbing nipples.

When he's satisfied with my squeak of discomfort, he relents and flicks the bells that are draped between my breasts on the leather cord. The melodic jingle mingles with his cruel laugh.

His hands close around my shoulders, and he drags me upright. With my hands bound behind me, I have to rely on his support to get to my feet. My torn dress slides down my body, pooling on the ground and leaving me bare before him. A scrap of black lace is my only bit of modesty, and judging by his possessive gaze, the lingerie only entices him more.

I glower at him, allowing the full force of my defiance to pierce him like a knife.

He simply smiles and caresses my cheek. "So beautiful. My pretty pet."

"Stop calling me that," I seethe.

He cocks his head at me, and midnight hair tumbles over the black skull mask. "Say the word, and this will end. You do have a choice, Abigail. Always. I'll never take that from you again."

My ire melts away. He's asking for my trust.

He said that he brought me here for a reason. He wants me to remember how good it can be between us when we both indulge in our mutual darkness. My soul matches his in so many ways.

My heart tugs toward his, stronger this time. I yearn for him, for us. I want to engage in this twisted game, but I'm frightened.

"I'm scared," I admit, my voice small.

His jaw firms, but his hand on my cheek remains achingly gentle. "I never want you to be scared of me."

"I'm scared of *me*. I shouldn't want this. It's sick and wrong."

"Nothing about you could ever be wrong. You're perfect, Abigail."

He tips my chin back so that he can stare down into my soul. "Do you want to stop?"

That question makes all the difference. I settle into my decision, accepting everything that we are. Accepting *him.*

And myself.

"No," I breathe. "I don't want to stop."

He leans in close, and his lips brush the shell of my ear when he commands, "Then run, little dove."

He steps back, watching me with open curiosity for my next move.

I straighten my shoulders and kick off my high heels. The dirt path is cool beneath my feet. The earth is hardpacked; it won't hurt my bare soles.

His tilted grin is pure, maniacal pleasure. "You have thirty seconds, and then I come after you."

"Aren't you going to untie my hands?"

"And let you pluck off those lovely bells? I don't think so."

I hesitate, torn between denying him his fun and wanting to unleash my most primal urges. This is a battle of wills, and even though there's no way I will win, I'm determined to engage in the fight. The struggle. The inevitable, ecstatic defeat.

"Twenty seconds now," he warns.

I start running. I have to get as far away as possible before slowing down; the damn bells will give me away if I continue sprinting, and I already know he's faster than I am.

I hurtle down the path, willing my eyes to adjust to the darkness as I run farther away from the light of the fountain. The maze opens up to my left, and I choose to take the turn rather than going straight. There's no way to know how to get to the exit, and Dane is well aware of that fact.

My fate is already sealed, but I grit my teeth and increase my speed.

He wants a hunt? I'll give him a hunt. He'll have to work for it if he wants to capture me.

With every pounding step, the bells sway on the cord between the silver clamps. The weight of them tugs at my trapped nipples as my breasts bounce. My blood runs hotter in my veins, and it's not just from the exertion of evading him. The torment to my nipples is unbearably erotic, and my inner thighs are wet with my arousal. My swollen labia throb with every stride, and I'm achingly aware of how empty I am without his cock filling me up.

"Abigail!" He roars my name from the center of the maze, and I know I'm out of time.

I duck down an opening to my right, winding my way deeper into the maze. I take turn after sharp turn, until I'm dizzy and my breath burns my lungs. He can clearly hear the jingling of the traitorous bells, but I think my path has been erratic enough to confuse him.

For a while, at least.

I slow down and struggle to breathe as shallowly as possible so that the bells won't jangle. My steps are light and careful, and I manage to take another turn without making a sound.

I'm not sure how long I manage to keep quiet before he calls out for me again.

"I know you're nearby, Abigail. Such a clever little pet. You're lost, but I'll find you."

He says the last like a mercy.

His voice is far too close. I have no choice: I have to start running again.

He barks a laugh when the bells chime, and a mix of defiant rage and desire heats my flushed cheeks.

His arrogance is galling, but my body craves him.

I deny my base, carnal needs and increase my speed, rounding another corner. Seconds later, I cry out before I can stop myself.

I've hit a dead end. And I can hear his heavy footfalls pounding closer.

I whirl, and his massive, shadowy form is barreling toward me, cutting off my exit. I scramble back, but I collide with the hedge. Branches prickle my bare skin, scratching my sensitized flesh like a sharp caress.

He slows as he closes in, and his white teeth flash in a feral smile through the darkness.

"Little dove," he coos. "Are you trapped?"

"Don't touch me," I snap, pressing myself deeper into the hedge.

"Poor little pet. All alone out here. So lost and afraid."

"I'm not afraid," I lie. Fear thrills through me in a tingling wave, setting all of my senses on high alert.

"You don't have to pretend with me." He says it like a reassurance that's belied by his mocking tone.

He's right in front of me, his massive body blocking any hope of escape.

"You seem to be caught in a snare. Let me help you."

He moves lighting fast, grasping my shoulders and tearing me away from the hedge. He tackles me to the ground, angling us so that his body takes the impact.

Then he rolls atop me, forcing me onto my front. The clamps bite into my nipples. With my hands bound behind me, there's nothing I can do but kick and scream.

My defiant shriek dies in my throat when I catch the glint of the blade out of the corner of my eye.

"Dane!" True, potent terror claws at my insides.

I crane my neck back so that I can keep the wickedly sharp hunting knife in my line of sight.

The last time he held a blade to my throat, he was the masked man. He terrorized me and violated me.

He's wearing a different skull mask now. The image of my alluring demon morphs into a horrific, macabre memory.

He strokes the length of my spine with his free hand and shushes me gently. The knife is nowhere near my skin; he's holding it at least two feet away from me, and it's pointed outward, not toward me.

"I took this fantasy from you," he rumbles. "I want to give it back."

My chest convulses on a shuddering breath. Terror still rides me hard, but his words touch something deep inside me.

He wants my consent. I could stop him right now if I wanted to.

But I don't speak. I don't use my safe word.

I want to take ownership of this fantasy too.

I close my eyes briefly and breathe through the worst of the clawing horror, until it subsides into fizzy, thrilling fear once again. I allow myself to sink into the giddy sensation, like I'm riding a roller-coaster.

I'm safe with Dane.

"Good girl," he praises. "So brave for me."

My eyes flutter open, and the blade glints in the moonlight as he slowly moves it closer to my body. When I don't scream or cringe away, he grasps my wrists with his other hand. The rope tugs slightly as he slips the knife through the knot.

I go utterly still.

"Be careful, little dove," he warns gently. "I don't want to accidentally clip your wings."

The blade slices upward, away from my body. The rope falls from my wrists, but I don't dare to move. I'm hardly breathing, and I'm becoming light-headed from lack of oxygen.

He shifts behind me, and I'm on my back.

The knife is still in his hand, and this time, the tip is pointed at my chest.

"Dane..." His name is little more than a pleading whisper.

"*Master*," he corrects me. "You're mine, Abigail. It's time you remembered what that means."

The knife flicks beneath the leather cord that connects the nipple clamps. The bells jingle softly as he slowly draws it upward on the flat of the blade.

"I wonder what will happen first," he muses, eyes glittering with cruel fascination. "Will the cord be severed, or will those tight little clamps be tugged off of your nipples?"

"Don't." I dread the pain of the latter threat.

"You do beg so sweetly, but that won't spare you. You're my helpless little plaything now. Mine to toy with however I want."

He slowly raises the knife, increasing the pressure on the cord. It begins to tug at the clamps, pulling on my abused nipples. Pain spears through me in sharp spikes that somehow turn to pure pleasure when they reach my core. I cry out and arch my back, desperate to alleviate the strain.

"Would you like that?" he taunts. "You could be my obedient little fucktoy. Or you can continue to suffer for me."

I growl through gritted teeth, the only sound I'm able to make when pain rakes at me, commanding most of my attention.

"You brought this on yourself,"

That's my only warning before he jerks the knife away from me. He doesn't turn it to sever the cord with the sharp edge. My scream fills the maze when the nipple clamps are yanked free. The searing shock of pain makes my vision flash white for an instant.

I blink rapidly, and tears stream down my temples to wet my hair. The world comes back into sharp focus when I see the knife hovering just above my stinging nipple.

Fear shudders through me, a primal response to danger.

"Please..."

"I would never damage your beautiful body," he reassures me. "But you're going to have to remain very still for me. I'll make the ache go away. I know you're hurting."

My nipples throb as though I've been stung by bees, but that doesn't ease my spike of terror when the cold flat of the blade touches one tight peak with the lightest pressure.

All of my muscles lock up tight. A small, pitiful whimper eases up my throat, but the tiny exhalation is the only move I dare to make.

He stares down at me, eyes dark pools in the shadows of his mask. His beautiful face is drawn into stony, merciless planes, and his cock is hard against my thigh.

He's getting off on this, reveling in his sadistic power over me.

And I'm molten for him.

My body relaxes, all of the fight going out of me as I submit. The blessed release of surrender is pure bliss, and it pulses through my body like a drug.

"So perfect," he breathes. "My Abigail."

"Yours." My lips shape the word, but I don't have enough air to speak. Not with the knife so perilously close to my vulnerable nipple.

He shifts the blade to my other breast, further soothing the sting from the clamps with cold steel. He keeps it there while he reaches between us, his free hand dipping under my soaked thong. He groans when he finds the wetness that coats my inner thighs.

"Stay just like that," he orders, and he sounds like he might be drugged too. "Don't move."

The knife is at my throat, sending a fresh burst of fear fluttering through my system. I float in it, riding the thrilling high.

I draw in shallow, careful breaths as he teases my swollen pussy with a featherlight touch.

"Please." I mouth the plea, but I'm no longer

begging for reprieve. I crave more: more fear, more pain, more pleasure.

I'll take everything he wants to do to me. I'll offer him anything he desires.

He's my dark god, my master.

My everything.

And he's looking at me like I'm the only person in his world. The only thing tethering him to sanity. He needs me so deeply that it transcends the bounds of physical lust. He yearns for me, just as I long for him, for this connection that we share.

Two thick fingers ease into my tight sheath, and he applies firm pressure to the sensitive spot inside me. The stimulation is slow, tender. So at odds with the violence of the knife at my throat.

My lashes flutter as primal chemicals mingle in my system. I'm no longer sure of the difference between fear and desire. There's only the burning need for him and the euphoric release of submission.

"Stay with me," he murmurs. "Keep breathing."

I realize I'm dizzy from lack of oxygen, so I draw in a careful breath. His will compels me, and I'm his to command. I'll do anything for him, suffer any torment. Because I know he'll give me exquisite ecstasy in return.

"Now, come for me."

He presses down on my clit and rubs my g-spot.

I don't have enough air to scream, and I don't dare to so much as writhe as cruelly potent pleasure rips through me. He watches me come in tormented silence, as though I'm the most fascinating, breathtaking thing he's ever seen.

The cold kiss of the blade is gone, and he tosses the knife far away from us. I immediately start shaking, my entire body trembling with the force of my residual fear.

He strokes my hair back from my sweat-slicked brow and crushes his lips to mine, devouring me. I groan into his mouth, a purely wanton sound.

I came only seconds ago, but I'm still throbbing for him. I crave him inside me, joining us in the most intimate way.

He can't seem to wait another moment, either. He unbuckles his belt and frees his cock. It presses at my slick opening, and I shift my hips up to welcome him. He slides in to the hilt, stretching me in one smooth thrust.

He breaks our kiss so that he can grasp my thighs. He directs me to lift my legs between us until my calves rest on his shoulders. He leans into me, and his cock sinks impossibly deeper, hitting a spot inside me that's almost painful. It adds the sweetest edge to our connection, and I tip my head back on a guttural moan.

I'm trapped beneath him, pinned by his strength. He grasps my wrists and holds them above my head. His other hand closes around my throat, squeezing gently.

He begins to claim me in long, hard thrusts that jar my entire body when he drives deep into me. My muscles coil tighter as my pleasure crests once again, and my inner walls clamp down on his cock. He snarls and increases his pace. With each possessive thrust, his fingers tighten around my throat incrementally.

Blood pounds in my ears, and the shadows of the maze draw closer. I can still breathe, but the pressure on my arteries restricts the blood flow to my brain.

"Scream for me," he growls. "Give me everything."

"Master!" I cry out, acknowledging his claim over me.

His title is a trigger, and my orgasm hits me with brutal force. Fireworks burst over my darkening world, and my scream fills the maze.

"Abigail!"

His cock pulses inside me, and for the first time, his hot cum lashes into me, marking me as his.

"I'm yours," I sob as bliss consumes me and the shadows lengthen.

Just before I float away entirely, he releases my throat. Oxygenated blood surges back to my brain, and the world turns surreal. The only thing tethering me to reality is Dane's soul-searing green gaze.

"Mine." He seals the promise with a fierce kiss.

21

DANE

It's past noon when Abigail finally stirs in my arms. She turns toward me, and her stunning, aquamarine eyes open. She offers me a lazy smile and stretches like a contented cat.

I marvel at her. I can hardly believe she's given herself to me after all of my crimes against her.

I was incapable of understanding how I'd wronged her until she showed me her powerful, disturbing self-portrait. She makes me see the world in ways I never thought possible. She is my world now. I'm no longer limited to my mundane, tedious existence when I experienced nothing but idle amusement in manipulating others. For the first time in my adult life, I care about someone other than myself.

Abigail is mine to covet, mine to shelter and protect. I'll do anything to keep her happy in my arms like she is right now.

Last night, she placed her full trust in me. I'll never betray that trust.

I press a kiss to her forehead. She hums happily and wraps her arms around me.

This might be the most perfect moment of my life.

"You need to eat," I murmur into her hair.

She cuddles closer. "Let's stay in bed for a while longer."

I can't deny her anything.

I'm not sure how long we hold each other in contented, companionable silence. This is how it's meant to be between us. This is how it will be. Every day for the rest of our lives.

"Daniel!"

Panic spikes through me, and I jolt upright.

That's my mother's shrill voice, echoing down the corridor.

No. She can't be here. James said he wouldn't tell our parents that I'm home.

But there are several sets of footsteps approaching my bedroom. Mum isn't alone.

I surge out of bed and quickly find my sweatpants, tugging them on to cover my nakedness.

"Who is that?" Abigail asks, her voice touched with alarm.

"Stay in here," I command.

I don't have time to explain.

I dart out of the bedroom and shut the door behind me, shielding Abigail from my family.

Dread is a lead weight in my stomach when I see both of my parents, flanked by my traitorous brother. I glower at him, and my fists clench at my sides.

"What the fuck, James? You said you wouldn't tell them I'm here."

His mouth is set in a grim line when he comes to a stop a few feet away from me. Just out of punching distance.

"That was before I knew you'd kidnapped Abigail."

"What?" The question is a touch breathless.

How can he know?

He sneers at me. "Do you think you have the monopoly on depravity in this family? And did you really think that mask was enough to conceal your identity last night?"

I rake a hand through my hair. This can't be happening.

"I heard her say that you kidnapped her. I heard her scream."

"Everyone else there knew it was just a game," I growl.

"They didn't see her after she wrecked my Jeep," he informs me coldly. "She was clearly desperate to get away from you that day. I thought you must've had a bad argument, but when I saw her last night, I finally got the full picture."

I fix him with the full force of my loathing. "Why couldn't you just ask us about this last night? Why didn't you talk to me about it like a man instead of tattling on me to our parents?"

James scoffs. "You had clearly coerced her into being at that party. I couldn't trust a word you said. And you carried her off somewhere before I could approach you. You left me with no choice."

I bare my teeth at him. "You didn't have to call *them.* You still could've come here on your own to ask me about it."

He shakes his head. "I am not Lord of this house yet. Dad is the one with the power to kick you out."

"What have you done this time, Daniel?" my mother demands shrilly. "And what on earth was that party you went to?" She rounds on James, including him in her censure. "Am I right in understanding that both of my sons attended some sort of sordid function last night? That you put the family name at risk of public scandal?"

James waves in dismissal, even though his cheeks flush. "Everyone was wearing masks," he says quickly. "We don't need to go into the details."

She narrows her pale blue eyes at him. "We will return to this conversation later." Her sharp gaze pins me again. "Explain yourself. Where is the woman you've supposedly kidnapped? Will she go quietly if we pay her? How much will your latest depravity cost this family?"

"I don't want your money," I bark. "I never have."

My father speaks up for the first time, his words slurring slightly from his chronic alcoholism. "We'll bail you out if we must," he asserts. "Just like all the other times. This will not get into the news cycle. You're still a Graham."

The prospect of accepting anything from them raises my ire. Especially when my father is the one talking about bailing me out. Just like all the times he's been bailed out of sticky situations to escape punishment for his crimes.

"I am not part of this family," I seethe. "I gave up the title."

"And yet, here you are," Mum accuses. "Making

yourself at home like the manor belongs to you. You're either in or you're out, Daniel. You've chosen to come back in. That means your actions reflect badly on the family. You will accept our money to pay off this woman. Make her go away."

"Abigail isn't going anywhere!" I thunder.

James is the only one with the good sense to take a step back from my volatility.

My mother and father remain coolly composed, completely unruffled by my uncharacteristic outburst. As though I'm still a child, and I'm incapable of controlling myself.

The awful memories that unlocked when I found Abigail bleeding in the wrecked Jeep rise up to take hold of my mind, my tongue.

"You think you can buy your way out of everything," I hiss at my father. "Just like you bribed the police not to arrest you for killing Katie. You murdered my sister, and you never paid for it."

"Daniel!" Mum's tone is a sharp rebuke. "You know we don't say that name in this house. It upsets your father."

"And you." I narrow my eyes at her. "You thought you could just replace my twin with another spare? With *him*?" I gesture sharply at James, and he pales.

"Let's just take a moment," he cajoles. "We can all have a cup of tea and talk about this rationally."

I bark a bitter laugh. "You think tea is going to help fix this? My sister is dead because of them. I watched her die. I was trapped with her dead body for hours, and none of you ever gave a shit."

"Really, Daniel." My mother sounds scandalized. "There's no need to make a scene. That was years ago. You're not a child anymore."

"I hate you." My tone goes cold and flat. "I thought I felt nothing for you at all, but I truly hate you. Stay the fuck away from me."

"You're the one who came back," my father reminds me with a scowl. "We didn't invite you here."

"I'm leaving," I snap. "I never want to see any of you ever again."

"I don't think so," Mum refuses. "You brought this mess to our doorstep. We're going to clean it up before anyone finds out what you've done. Now, where is this woman you've kidnapped?"

She says it with irritation, not horror. She's not remotely surprised or bothered by the fact that I could commit such a crime. It's simply the optics she's worried about.

Everything for appearances.

"I'm right here."

I whirl and find Abigail standing in the open doorway to my bedroom.

"You can't be out here," I say, gentling my tone when I address her. "Go back inside. I'll handle this."

The last thing I want is to subject her to the cruelty of my relatives. She's already suffered so much at the hands of her own parents. I'll shield her from mine.

My brave, stubborn Abigail lifts her chin and steps up beside me. She fixes my family with an imperious stare and takes my hand in hers.

"I'm with Dane willingly," she asserts.

My heart skips a beat.

Last night, she gave herself to me willingly, but until this moment, I wasn't sure of her loyalty. I wasn't certain that she wouldn't try to leave me again if she had the opportunity to be free of me.

I never intended to give her that choice, but I still didn't know if she would challenge me over it.

"I'm sorry we came here unannounced." Her voice is frosty as she continues to address my parents. She's perfectly poised and icily polite. "We'll leave now."

"Wait just a minute!" Mum insists, bristling at the challenge. "My son isn't going anywhere." She looks at me again, eyes glittering with accusation. "Do you know how difficult it's been to excuse your absence for all these years? To conceal our estrangement? You've come home, and now you're staying."

"You're distressed," Abigail remarks coolly. "I understand. It must be very difficult to have a son who hates you. Maybe you should go have that cup of tea while we pack. I've heard it's good for the nerves."

My mother's face has gone beet red, and she splutters, "You... How dare... In my own home?"

"Americans." My father spits out the word like a curse, a condemnation. "Bloody upstarts."

"Yes, I'm sure we'll all be happy to part ways," Abigail continues smoothly. "Dane and I just need a few minutes to collect our things. Then we'll be out of your hair." She pointedly glances at my father's balding head.

I grin. She's good at this.

I lost my composure, and my fierce pet has come to my defense.

How could I ever deserve this woman?

"Come on." James finally speaks up again. "Let's have that cuppa. Now, Mum."

He gently grasps our mother's shoulder and turns her away from me.

"Dad," he calls back over his shoulder as they head for the stairs. "I'm sure there's a bottle of whisky somewhere in the kitchen."

The promise of alcohol moves him like nothing else. My father gives me one final contemptuous sneer. Then he turns and walks away too.

I turn to my woman, my miracle, and trace the curve of her amethyst curl that fascinates me endlessly.

"Thank you," I say. I don't have the words to express the depth of my gratitude, my admiration.

She waves off my thanks. "You're welcome. They deserved it. Now, we need to get the hell out of here. Do you have your own car?"

I nod and trail her into the bedroom to pack. Wherever Abigail goes, I'll follow.

22

ABIGAIL

"It's so beautiful," I gush, spinning in a circle to take in the stunning, historic city of York. "I can't believe you grew up here. It's magical."

Dane is staring at me, not the imposing, centuries-old Minster. I've been studying the intricately carved masonry, and my fingers itch for my paintbrush. I'm not sure when I'll have the opportunity to express this scene on my canvas, so I'm doing my best to commit it to memory.

"Yes," he says softly. "I suppose it is a bit magical."

"A bit?" I tease. "There are medieval buildings lining every cobbled street. It doesn't seem real. It's like we've stepped back into another time."

His mouth tips in a lopsided smile that makes my heart flutter. "Is it?"

He gestures at the man who's painted in purple from head-to-toe, trying his best to remain stationary on a bike.

I've seen better human statues, and I can't suppress a giggle. Dane isn't remotely impressed by the man.

I decide to include the street performer in my painting. The juxtaposition with the historic Minster is whimsical, charming. I'll try to capture Dane's expression of pure bafflement too.

I loop my arm through his, steering us away from the spectacle. "You just don't understand art."

"That's not art."

"You have to open your mind," I urge, but I'm only half-serious. Bantering with him is fun. "Anything can be art."

He scoffs. "Now you're just making up meaningless platitudes. There is no comparison between your work that that purple man."

"Beauty is in the eye of the beholder." I shrug.

He pauses and urges me to face him. One dexterous hand brushes my hair back from my cheek. "There's only one beautiful thing I see here."

I flush with pleasure and cut my gaze away, flustered.

He cups my jaw, urging me to tip my head back so that I have no choice but to look up at him.

"You are the most stunning, remarkable woman I've ever met," he says solemnly. "The way you defended me in front of my parents..." He trails off for a moment and traces the shape of my lips with his thumb. "I can never express what that means to me. How proud I am to call you *mine*."

"They were being cruel to you," I say quietly. "I would do it again a hundred times over. I won't let them hurt you anymore."

His eyes flash with green fire. "And I won't let your parents hurt you," he vows in return. "When we get back to Charleston, I'll make sure they won't bother you."

My heart lifts. "We're going back to Charleston?"

He nods. "I booked our tickets from London. We fly out in a week. I know you want to go home, but there's something I want to show you in York first."

"What is it?" I ask.

I don't mind the short delay. The promise that we're going home is enough for me. I trust Dane to keep his word.

I'm not sure what my life will look like when I

return to Charleston—the small, quiet little life I built for myself after college is over now. Dane forcibly removed me from it, but I no longer feel resentment over his decision to take me away. I understand him now. Despite everything, I've chosen him.

He respects me and treats me as his equal. If anything, he reveres me and places my needs above his own.

"It's just there," Dane answers me, pointing at a large red building with white accents.

It looks Victorian, and it probably is. Dane said the Romans were the first to build York's city walls. The Victorian period came nearly two millennia after, even if that era seems like a long time ago to my American sensibilities. Everything in York is frozen in its own time period.

I sigh and lean into Dane, admiring the beauty of our surroundings all over again as we walk the short distance to the red building.

When we approach the front door, I notice the sign in large gold lettering: The Howard Gallery. Dane is indulging my love of art, even though I know he doesn't connect with it the way I do.

"Thank you." I squeeze his hand in a pulse of gratitude as we enter the building.

"Don't thank me yet."

I shoot him a puzzled look, but before I can ask what he means, a tall, slender man in a waistcoat steps into our path.

He's probably in his late twenties, with sandy blond hair and understated, round glasses with a thin wire rim. He offers me a warm smile.

"You're Abigail Foster?" He extends a hand. "I'm Stephen Lansing."

"It's nice to meet you," I reply automatically, even though I'm somewhat taken aback by his familiarity.

"Dane Graham." Dane's voice is a touch cool when he introduces himself, and he's eyeing Stephen's hand grasping mine.

The younger man quickly releases me to shake Dane's hand instead. "Yes, we spoke on the phone. It's good to meet you in person. I'll be your point of contact at the gallery."

Dane doesn't look impressed. "Shouldn't Abigail be speaking to the owner?"

Stephen lifts his chin. "My father is very busy. He trusts me to manage the collection. I just finished my PhD at the University of York. I'm more than qualified."

"I'm sure you are," I say politely. "Would you

mind explaining how you know who I am? I'm a little lost here."

Stephen glances from me to Dane and back again.

"This is a surprise," Dane explains. Then he turns to me. "Your work will be on display here starting this week. It will remain in the gallery for the summer."

I gape at him, then manage to ask, "What work? All of my paintings are back in Charleston."

Stephen looks confused. "You sent pictures," he says to Dane. "The three paintings of the Yorkshire Dales and the self-portrait."

I blink at Dane. "You didn't."

He grins at me. "I did."

My heart lifts. I've never been featured in a gallery before. And I never would've submitted those pieces for consideration myself. I felt they were imperfect, nothing special.

A troubling thought occurs to me.

Dane arranged this. Not me.

I didn't get here on merit.

"How much does it cost?" I ask Stephen, and Dane's hand tightens in a vise around mine.

"Cost?" Stephen is completely befuddled by this entire interaction. "If you choose to sell the paintings to interested buyers, you can name your price. We take a ten percent commission."

"No," I correct him. "I mean, how much did it cost for you to agree to feature my work?"

"I didn't pay him, Abigail," Dane says, voice rough with frustration.

And maybe a touch of hurt.

Oh.

"I'm sorry." I look at Dane when I apologize and brush my thumb over his palm. "I didn't understand the arrangement. Thank you for submitting my work." I turn a friendly smile on Stephen. "I'm thrilled to have my work in your gallery. What do you need from me?"

He returns my smile easily. "Come by sometime tomorrow after close, and we can discuss how you would like your paintings displayed. Is eight o'clock too late for you?"

"Not at all," I confirm. "Eight sounds perfect."

I truly am thrilled to have my work in a real art gallery for the first time in my life, but I'm mostly preoccupied with worry that I've upset Dane.

"I'll see you then," I promise, ending the meeting so that I can be alone with him.

I'll prove to him just how much this means to me.

"I'm sorry." I apologize as soon as we're in the privacy of our rented penthouse.

The view through the floor-to-ceiling windows is stunning. The city of York with its historic architecture is defined by the Minster and Clifford's Tower, the remnants of a Norman castle. We can see for miles beyond the city walls, all the way out to the rolling green hills of the Yorkshire countryside.

But for now, the scene doesn't hold my attention like it did when we checked in several hours ago. I'm too concerned that I've hurt Dane.

"There's no need to apologize," he reassures me, but tension lingers around his jaw.

"I shouldn't have assumed that you paid for me to be featured in the gallery. I know that bothered you."

He caresses my cheek, and I'm easily forgiven.

"Your work speaks for itself," he assures me. "They were all too eager to feature you. If you do choose to sell, I'm sure they'll earn a hefty commission. Although, I would like to request that we keep the self-portrait."

My brow furrows. "Why? Doesn't it disturb you?"

I place my hand over his heart, securing our

connection as we both think back to the painful day when I showed him the painting of my anguish.

"No," he replies firmly. "It's the most powerful piece of art I've ever seen. You deserve to share your talent with the world. You deserve to be seen. Celebrated. Your paintings will be in galleries in London and New York. We can travel anywhere you need to go to establish your career. I know you have difficulty accepting my money, but let me do this for you, at least. I'm sure you'll have plenty of your own funds soon enough."

My heart soars, and my eyes sting with a swell of emotion that I fear I recognize.

It's too soon to say it, but I've felt it growing in me every day since he dropped to his knees and said he can't live without me.

It would be so easy to love Dane again.

I think I already do.

But I need to assert my independence first. I need to go back home and build a new life for myself, one that I share with him.

"All I want is to start my own gallery in Charleston," I say instead. "I don't need London or New York. I just want to be home."

I want to put down roots, to feel the security of a

home that I never experienced in the house where I was raised.

I think I can have that with Dane. We can share a home together. The first one either of us has ever truly known.

He curves my purple curl around his finger. “Home,” he agrees. “We’re going home. You’ll have your gallery, Abigail.”

“It’s just a loan,” I say firmly. “I’ll pay you back.”

He shakes his head. “What’s mine is yours.”

I lift my chin. “I don’t have any money to offer now, but the same goes for you. Anything I earn, I’ll share with you. We’re equals, Dane.”

He cups my nape, drawing me closer. “No, we’re not. You are so much more than I could ever be.”

He crushes his lips to mine, consuming my soft gasp. He worships me with his mouth, his tongue, his teeth. I belong to him, but I’ve never felt freer than I do in this moment. Empowered. Cherished.

I kiss him back, matching his intensity as I silently pledge my love to him in return.

We move into the bedroom in a frenzy, tearing at each other’s clothes. By the time he tosses me onto the bed, I’m naked. He fixes me with a wolfish grin and steps out of his jeans.

He towers over me, completely bare and glorious

as a god. His powerful body is so much stronger than mine will ever be.

But I hold my own, softer power over him.

I extend my hand, beckoning him to join me on the bed. He grasps it and kisses my palm.

"One moment, pet."

He steps away, and I whine, "I need you, Dane."

He smirks at me as he rummages in his duffel bag. "So impatient. You'll get my cock in your tight cunt soon enough. I want to play with you first."

When he returns to the bed, he's holding a long coil of rope. Anticipatory pleasure races over me in a light shiver.

I love when he ties me up so that I'm helpless to resist him.

But I'm craving something sweeter today, something more sensual.

"I don't want to fight you," I admit. "I just want us to be together."

He drops a kiss on my forehead. "I'm feeling the same way, little dove."

"Then why do you need the rope?"

"Because even though you're not going to struggle, I'm still in control. And I want to bind you."

I huff out a breath, but I'm not really exasperated. "So selfish," I tease.

"Don't worry. I'll still make you come so hard that you'll weep in gratitude. I'll always take care of you."

I release a contented hum. "I know. I trust you."

He climbs onto the king-size bed with me and grasps my waist, dragging me to the center of the mattress.

"Kneel," he commands.

I obey easily. I have no desire to challenge him today. I simply want to please him. And to be worshipped in return.

"Put your hands behind your head, and keep them there."

When I'm in the position he desires, he settles behind me. His thighs are on either side of my own, and his broad chest cradles my back. He presses one big hand to my sternum, urging me to lean into his strength.

I melt against him with a sigh.

"Breathe with me," he murmurs, nuzzling my hair and inhaling my scent.

Salt-kissed cedarwood enfolds me, and I relax deeper into his embrace.

Our chests rise and fall as one as we take deep, even breaths together.

My heartbeat is slow and steady beneath his hand. I wonder if his matches mine.

A sense of intimacy blossoms between us. I've experienced carnal bliss with him many times, but this bond is so intense that it's almost painful. My body hums for him, but I'm not throbbing with desperate lust. I could simply stay in this peaceful space with him for an eternity.

We drift for a while, and my eyes slide closed as my head drops back against his shoulder. He presses tender kisses along the column of my throat, warming my body with simmering desire.

His broad palm remains pressed over my heart. His other hand is wrapped in rope, and when he drags his knuckles beneath my breasts, the slightly rough hemp stimulates my sensitized skin. I'm hyperaware of him, and my nerves sparkle and dance everywhere the rope grazes me.

I release all of the lingering tension in my body on a low moan and surrender to him completely.

"Good girl," he praises. "Such a sweet pet."

The rope wraps around my chest in a slow, sensual embrace. His hands never break contact with my skin while he binds me. We're constantly connected, melting into one another.

My heart beats for his.

The rope winds around my chest, knotting in an intricate pattern that I can't quite follow. Dane handles me with quiet confidence, and I simply allow myself to be with him.

I don't have to fight. I don't have to say anything.

All I have to do is remain where he's positioned me and breathe with him, just as he's commanded.

But as the rope coils tighter, my chest is constricted incrementally. I try to match his breaths, but my lungs can't fully expand beneath the steady pressure of the rope cage he's weaving around me.

"Dane." I pant his name and draw in a sip of oxygen.

"Your body is mine," he intones, tugging the rope a fraction tighter. "Your breath is mine." Another tug, another shallow breath. "Your pleasure is mine."

"Yes," I whisper.

I've entered an almost meditative state. All that exists is my breath and his hands on the ever-tightening rope.

My lashes flutter, and my mind floats.

The pressure stops increasing, but the tension doesn't ease. He ties off his work, leaving me in the restrictive embrace of his cruelly sensual rope.

He hasn't bound my limbs at all. I could try to

run away if I wanted to. I could try to free myself from his knots.

But I'm thoroughly subdued by his will. I submitted as soon as his hand settled over my heart.

He gently grasps my wrists and directs my arms to drop. "On your hands and knees."

The murmured order sinks into me, and I float into position. As I move my body, the rope shifts around me in a tight caress. His hand settles on my back, stroking the length of my spine, and I arch into his touch.

My pleasure is warm and pleasant, like a perfect summer morning on a pristine beach. I bask in it, reveling in the beauty of the perfect moment with him.

His touch trails lower, tracing my swollen, aching folds. I'm wet and ready for him, and he growls his satisfaction when he tests the slickness between my legs.

He takes his time toying with me, playing with me like he has all the time in the world to explore my pussy. He seems intent on memorizing each of my shallow sighs and quiet whimpers in response to his teasing touch.

My body hums for him, bliss illuminating every

inch of my flesh until I'm incandescent with pleasure.

"Master." My lips form his title, but barely any sound escapes from my restricted chest. "Master, Master, Master..."

It's beyond an orgasm. There is no building tension, no vicious, cresting wave of ecstasy. I am a being of pure pleasure, endless and complete.

He plays with all of me, exploring my ass as well as my pussy. He tests me, entering me in teasing strokes before pushing deeper. Stretching wider.

Something cool and wet drops onto my asshole, and I shudder at the intensity of carnal sensation when my body is alight with sensual awareness.

A larger intrusion presses against my tight hole, and I know it's not his finger this time.

"Relax," he coaxes. "You can take the plug. I want to fill you up while I fuck your cunt."

I've never experienced anything like this, but I trust him implicitly. My body softens to accommodate the intrusion. He slowly pumps it into me in slow, short strokes, stretching me wider with each gentle thrust. Pain edges my pleasure, and my fingers curl into the sheets.

"Almost there," he urges. "Good girl. Take it for me."

He tweaks my clit with his other hand, and my inner muscles contract. The plug slips into me fully, and the pain abates as it settles deep inside me.

The penetration is strange, but not entirely uncomfortable. And as he continues to stroke my clit, the pleasure that fills my entire being begins to concentrate at my core.

"Are you ready for me, pet?"

"Always," I whisper.

He kneels behind me and lines his hard cock up with my wet pussy. Now that he's almost inside me, I'm desperate for him to fill me. He enters me in one long, slow slide, then stills. I lift my hips in wanton invitation for more, and his fingers dig into my butt, holding me still with a bite of bruising pain.

He stretches me wide open and simply stares down at me, indulging in the lewd sight of the toy filling my ass while his cock is buried deep inside me.

I begin to quiver. I've never felt so unbearably full, and the erotic stimulation is becoming too intense to bear.

He taps on the base of the plug, and I cry out as forbidden pleasure shudders through me. It undulates through my core, and my inner walls contract around him.

He hisses out a sharp curse, and his fingers flex into my tender flesh.

Finally, mercifully, he starts to move inside me. His cockhead drags across my g-spot, and I shake with the force of the ecstasy that rolls through me in relentless waves. Each time he thrusts deep, he pushes on the base of the plug. He lays claim to my body, just as he promised from the very beginning.

Tears gather at the corners of my eyes; the strength of my emotions is too intense for me to contain them within myself.

He takes me in a merciless rhythm, using my body for his own pleasure. I'm lost in a flood of euphoria, and I fall out of time and place. All that exists is Dane.

My dark god.

My protector.

My master.

He comes undone on a roar, and his hot seed lashes into me, branding me. His name shudders from my constricted chest on a choked cry.

He catches me as my muscles give out, holding me beneath him to keep us joined for a few moments longer.

"No," I whimper when he finally pulls out.

He shushes me gently. "I promised to take care of

you," he reminds me. "You need to breathe properly."

His hands are on me again, tugging at the rope.

"I've got you," he promises, slowly uncoiling the length from around my body.

As it loosens, my breaths come deeper, slower. I remain cocooned in my transcendent state, on my own personal plane of being where only Dane and I exist.

He holds me, his massive body enfolding mine from behind. The rope has fallen away entirely, and his hand has returned to my heart.

We breathe together in perfect time, our souls a perfect match.

23

ABIGAIL

"That's perfect." Stephen grins at me and scrawls a final note on his tablet. "I think the lighting here will really make your landscapes pop."

We've spent the last two hours walking through the gallery and reviewing the best placements for my paintings. I'm deeply gratified at the time he's putting into making the arrangements. It's nearly ten PM.

"I've kept you too long," I say. "If that's everything, I'll get out of here so you can lock up."

"It's been a pleasure getting to know you better," he replies, dismissing my assertion that I've taken up too much of his evening. "And it's always exciting to meet an emerging talent. We're lucky to be the first gallery to feature your work."

My cheeks heat, and I duck my head. "That's very kind of you to say."

"I mean it." He sounds sincere. "Come to the office with me for a minute. We'll have a drink to celebrate. I have a beautiful fifteen-year-old whisky. Do you like whisky?"

"Not really," I equivocate. I don't know if it feels entirely appropriate to have a drink at the gallery. "I like sweeter drinks."

His broad smile doesn't waver, and he gives me a conspiratorial wink. "Don't tell anyone, but I do too. I have plenty of soft drinks we can use as mixers."

"With your nice whisky?" I attempt a polite way to decline his invitation. "Isn't that basically a crime in the U.K.?"

He laughs. "I think it's considered a crime anywhere in the world, but I can keep a secret."

"All right," I capitulate. "Just a little splash for me, please. I really don't like the taste of alcohol."

This is my first big break, and I don't want to offend the young man who's taking a chance on me. His father owns this gallery. It reeks of nepotism, but I've been genuinely impressed by Stephen's knowledge and eye for detail. I'm confident leaving my work in his capable hands for the summer.

I follow him back to his office, and I wish I had my phone to text Dane that I'll be late. He's expecting me back at the penthouse around this time, and I don't want him to worry.

But my phone battery died weeks ago. Dane didn't bother to bring the correct charger from America once he messaged my friends to allay their concerns.

He's assured me that I'll have my phone back as soon as we return to Charleston, so I haven't been too concerned about it.

But it would be good to text him now. I'd rather not have him break into the gallery to get to me if he thinks I've stayed too late.

Even as I think it, a small smile plays around my lips. He might be overbearing at times, but my fiercely possessive lover would do anything to protect me.

Still, it's best to make this a very quick celebratory drink.

I don't actually want Dane to kick down the door.

"Please, sit." Stephen gestures at the small couch in the cramped but tastefully furnished office.

I oblige him, sitting down while he goes behind the desk to retrieve his stashed whiskey.

"Just a tiny splash," I reiterate when he pulls out a half-empty bottle.

His brow furrows, and he looks confused for a moment. Then he smacks his hand to his forehead.

"Idiot," he mumbles. He offers me a rueful smile. "The cups are in the kitchen with the soft drinks. I hope you don't mind a mug."

"You really don't have to go to all this trouble," I say, giving him an out. "I'm fine without a drink."

"We have to toast to your success," he insists. "I'll be right back."

True to his word, he's gone for less than two minutes before he returns with two mugs filled with soda. One has a pug dog with a monocle, and the other features kittens dancing on a rainbow.

"Dog or cats?" Stephen asks.

"Cats, please."

He tips the tiniest splash of whiskey into my requested mug. That amount of alcohol should be easily manageable. The ride back to the penthouse will take less than ten minutes, and there's a taxi rank right outside the gallery. I can get back to Dane quickly once I down this drink.

"We used to have a mug that said, 'Gough hard

or Gough home,' but I smashed it last week," Stephen says as he presses the kitten mug into my hand.

Our fingers brush accidentally, and I almost spill my drink in my haste to withdraw from the awkward moment.

"Sorry," he says with a shaky laugh. "I always get nervous around beautiful women. I'm talking bollocks."

That comment makes me more uncomfortable, so I edge away from Stephen and take a gulp of whisky-tinged soda. It's sweet and goes down easily.

"Ah, shit," he continues. "I'm being awkward as fuck. I'm sorry. I spend so much time working at the gallery that I think I'm forgetting how to socialize like a normal person."

I offer him a polite smile. There's no need to antagonize him after all the work he's putting in for my art, but I won't encourage him, either.

"Have you worked here long?" I make small talk instead of reassuring him that his comment was acceptable. "You said you recently finished your PhD, right?"

I take another big sip of my drink. I don't want to appear like I'm rushing to get away from him, but Dane really will start to get worried soon.

And I'm liking Stephen less and less with every passing minute.

His eyes flick to my lips and then back to my eyes. I pretend I didn't notice, but I let my smile drop.

"Yeah," he replies, chest puffing with pride. "I'm Dr. Lansing now. You know, I have a lot of connections in London. Some of my uni mates live there now. I could make some calls if you want."

I take another sip of my sweet drink. I wish Stephen had put some ice in the mugs. It's too warm in this cramped office, even though the temperature must be dropping outside.

"That's okay, but thank you." I refuse his offer. "I have plans to open my own gallery in Charleston. I won't have time to travel to London."

"There's no need to be coy." His voice drops deeper, and I don't trust the slightly husky edge to his words. "I'm happy to help you out."

My mug is over half-empty now, thank goodness. I'm ready to leave. I don't like how pushy he's being, even if he has helped me a lot today.

"Like I said, I don't have the time. But I appreciate the offer."

My skin is getting sticky with perspiration. I really should step outside sooner rather than later.

"Are you okay?" Stephen asks, brow furrowed with concern.

Heat rolls beneath the surface of my skin in a nauseating wave.

"Actually, I'm feeling a little lightheaded," I admit. "I need some fresh air."

"Drink some more. It'll cool you down. And it's mostly soda. The sugar should help."

I suppose I haven't eaten enough tonight, since this meeting is running far later than planned. Sugary soda isn't going to help all that much, but I drain the last of my drink anyway. I'm so hot, and I need to get outside into the cooler night air.

"Stay for a little while longer," he cajoles. "We should talk more about your career."

He slides out of focus for a second.

I'm more than just lightheaded. I'm getting dizzy.

I wish I could call Dane to come pick me up.

I close my eyes and draw in a deep breath, willing the room to stop spinning.

"You should let me make those London calls." Stephen is still talking to me, but his voice sounds oddly far away. "I really can help you out."

His hand is on my knee.

What the hell?

My eyes snap open, and I surge to my feet.

The world tilts, and Stephen catches my elbow to steady me.

"Whoa." He laughs. "Steady on. How much of a lightweight are you? I knew you Americans can't hold your drink, but this is ridiculous."

I shake my head. "You said it was just a splash. I saw you..." My tongue is thick in my mouth. "I saw you pour it."

I'm on the couch again. Stephen's leg is pressed against mine. He brushes his hand over my hot cheek and tucks my hair behind my ear.

"You really are beautiful," he says. "And so talented. Any man would be lucky to have you."

"I'm with Dane." My fierce declaration comes out soft and slurred. "Get away from me."

His hand is on my thigh. "Your boyfriend doesn't have to know. This is our secret, right? You agreed."

I shake my head again, and the room spins. "I didn't. Just a drink."

"You're talented, but you won't get ahead in your career without the right connections. I'm a useful person to know. We should have a good relationship."

"No." It's all I can manage when everything is swirling around me.

Cool air hits my chest.

"You're so flushed," Stephen says as he parts another button on my blouse.

I try to bat his hands away, but he easily brushes me off.

"Stop." It's little more than a slurred whisper.

My stomach churns, heightening my nausea.

The cool air caressing my bare stomach is a blissful relief from the heat that's surging beneath my skin. I groan at the sweet reprieve, and my muscles relax.

"That's better," Stephen praises. "I knew you could be friendly. There's no need to be so uptight."

Tears wet my lashes, blurring the spinning world.

Dane. I want Dane.

The hands that are touching me are all wrong. The fingers are slenderer, the palms slick and clammy. He gropes at me without finesse, exploring my body for his own pleasure rather than mine.

My eyes slide closed, and my low moan of despair fills the cramped office.

24

DANE

The sign on the gallery door is flipped to *closed*, but the door is unlocked. Abigail must still be here with Stephen.

Irritation tightens my jaw. She was supposed to return to the penthouse nearly twenty minutes ago. I've tried to give her space to work—I have to respect her independence—but I can't wait any longer.

I should've given her a damn phone so I can reach her whenever I want.

Or I should've just accompanied her to her meeting at the gallery. I should've stayed by her side, where I can watch over her. I should keep her on a leash so that she's never out of my sight.

I shake my head sharply and push open the

door. She won't thank me if I burst into her meeting like an enraged, possessive brute.

But I can't bring myself to put on my civilized mask, either.

Stephen will have to deal with the cold, clinical monster at my core. It's the best I can do at the moment when all I want is to punish him for keeping Abigail from me.

I walk through the gallery, searching for them. The lights are still on, but I don't hear their voices echoing from any of the spacious rooms.

I scowl and find a narrow corridor on the ground floor that's marked *staff only*. They must be somewhere in the back offices.

Just the thought of that little fucker being alone with Abigail in private makes white-hot rage pulse through my veins.

I remind myself that she won't like it if I punch the gallery owner's son in his entitled rich kid face. No matter how much I would enjoy smashing those pretentious glasses with my fists.

A low moan rolls from the back office, and I immediately know it's hers. I live for that sound.

And she's making it for another man.

My chest hollows out, and the ground shifts beneath my feet.

This can't be real. She wouldn't.

She gave herself to me.

The corridor blurs around me as I surge toward them. All of my muscles coil tight, ready to unleash my fury in a burst of violence.

I storm into the office, and my stomach drops at the sight of them together on the small couch.

She's beneath him, her blouse unbuttoned. His hands are on her breasts, and his lips taste hers.

He'll die for this. And Abigail...

I'll think about her punishment later.

Because I can never hurt her. Never.

Back in her studio, I offered her the heart from my chest. She might as well have ripped it out with her bare hands.

I bellow at the agony of her betrayal.

Him. I focus on *him.* He'll suffer and scream before I end his miserable life.

He tears his lips from hers, and his brown eyes are wide behind his large glasses when he sees me surging toward him.

"Wait!" he gasps, but he'll get no mercy from me.

I grab him by his shirt and yank him off of her before tossing him across the room like garbage. His filthy hands touched her. His taint mars her perfect skin.

He scrambles away from me, but there's nowhere for him to go. I lash out, my boot connecting with his jaw. It shatters at the impact, and he screams. I stomp my heel down on the back of the hand that touched what's mine. The fine bones crunch beneath my heel.

Before I can destroy his other hand, Abigail moans again.

In horror at my violence?

I stiffen. I shouldn't be affected by her fear. She should be afraid of me.

I'm the monster out of her worst nightmares. I always have been.

"Dane..." My name is slow and oddly slurred.

I whirl to face her, panic spiking through my system. Did I injure her somehow when I tore that bastard off of her? Even in my rage, the thought makes my stomach lurch with a surge of nausea.

Her lovely eyes are unfocused and strangely dull. It's inherently *wrong*. She's peering at me like she can't quite see me.

She's sprawled out on the couch exactly as she was when I stormed in. She hasn't tried to cover herself. She hasn't moved at all.

Her hand twitches toward me, and her soft whimper of distress shreds me.

A red haze descends over my vision.

He drugged my Abigail. He touched her. He violated her.

And I failed to protect her.

So many men have wanted my beautiful pet. Sick bastards who would do anything just to touch her. Taste her. Fuck her.

Whether she wants them or not.

I may be a monster, but I'm *her* monster.

I grasp her chilled hand and brush my lips over her knuckles.

"I've got you," I promise. "You're safe."

Behind me, Stephen groans through his broken jaw.

I carefully button her blouse so that she's covered, hiding her from his covetous eyes.

The eyes that I'm about to pluck out.

"Don't watch, Abigail," I command softly, stroking her hair back from her cheek. Her lashes flutter. "That's it. Close your eyes for me. I'll take care of this. I'll take care of you,"

I drop a kiss on her lips, and they're far too still beneath mine.

Rage surges back to the fore, and I round on my enemy.

He's crawling away from me, dragging himself

along the aged cream carpet with his unbroken hand.

I smash his delicate bones with my heel, ensuring he'll never hold a pen again.

Not that he'll need to.

He'll be dead within minutes.

A savage rush soars through my system, and if it weren't for Abigail's distress, I would bark a cruel laugh at the incredible high. As it is, I focus my righteous fury on the only thing that matters now: making him suffer in the short time he has left.

I surrender to the red haze, and I take out my retribution in blood.

When I return to Abigail, my hands are coated in gore. I frown down at them. I can't let his filthy blood mar her body.

Now that I'm coming down from my vicious high, some of my rationality is returning.

There's a dead body to deal with.

Ron was so easy to dispose of. Back in Charleston, the natural predator had done all the work for me. The alligator didn't leave any trace of him behind.

But this...

Stephen is a bloody mess in a gallery in the

middle of York. I hope to fuck there's not a camera in this office.

Probably not, since he won't have wanted a recording of what he was doing to Abigail.

My fists clench at my sides, and I wish I could kill him all over again.

I take a breath and force myself to think.

I'll have to leave Stephen here. I don't have a hope of dragging his body anywhere to dispose of it; there are too many tourists in the city for me to get him very far without someone screaming.

There will be an investigation once his body is found in the gallery, but there's nothing concrete to link me to the crime. I had reason to be in this building only yesterday. If I've left any small traces of myself behind, they can be easily explained away.

I inspect my hands. None of the blood is mine. My heavy boots did most of the work until I squeezed the last of the life out of him.

I'll have to dispose of the boots. And my clothes. I'll drop them in the river later.

Luckily, I'm dressed in a black shirt and dark wash jeans. The blood that's splattered my clothes won't be easily visible when I step outside into the night.

I'm no forensic expert. I might be missing something, but if I get the hell out of the country as soon as possible, I won't be around for the police to question me.

I have to get Abigail back to the safety of the penthouse. As soon as she wakes up tomorrow, we'll leave. London is only a couple of hours away. We can be on a flight by tomorrow night.

I lift her limp body and cradle her close to my chest.

"You're safe," I promise. "Everything will be okay."

25

DANE

Abigail stirs in my arms with a groan. I shush her and pull her closer, stroking her silken hair to soothe her.

Warm tears wet my chest, and she sobs softly.

"You're all right," I promise. "We're back at the penthouse. I've got you."

Her delicate body convulses in a violent shudder.

"He can't hurt you." I can't quite keep the growl from roughening my reassurance. "He'll never touch you again."

"What happened?" she asks, shaking against me. "We had one drink. I was so hot and dizzy. And then..."

My throat is too tight to speak. Her distress shreds me.

My failure to protect her twists my insides into painful knots.

"Did he..." She chokes on the question. "I don't remember..."

I force myself to say, "When I got to you, his hands were on you, but he was fully dressed."

She blinks up at me. "So you...got to me in time?"

I manage a jerky nod.

It hadn't been in time. Not at all.

He'd groped her and stripped off her shirt. He'd imprinted his taint onto her creamy skin.

She wraps her arms around me, clinging on to me like I'm her anchor in the storm.

I don't deserve it, but I'm selfish enough to cage her in my own embrace.

"I wanted you so desperately," she murmurs against my neck. "I wanted to leave."

The words should be a balm to my ravaged heart, but all I feel is shame searing my chest.

For an insane, agonized moment, I'd thought she was with him willingly. I'd assumed the worst because deep down, I've always known I'm not worthy of her.

I've craved her too much to care about my unworthiness.

I wanted her, so I took her. I made her mine, whether she consented or not.

She's still mine.

I can't let her go, no matter how undeserving I am.

"We're at the penthouse?" she asks, peering around to get her bearings. "Why?"

"Because it's the safest place for you. As soon as you feel ready to travel, we'll go back to Charleston. We can be in London in two hours for the flight."

"I mean..." She shakes her head as though to clear it. "Where are the police? Didn't you report Stephen for what he did to me?"

A shadow of my righteous rage tightens my muscles. "I'm sure the police are dealing with him now."

They'll have found his dead body this morning. He's in a body bag, already rotting.

"Is it okay for us to go back to Charleston now?" she presses. "Won't the police want to talk to me?"

I contemplate her for a moment, debating how much to tell her. She'll probably be upset if I tell her Stephen is dead, but I also don't want to lie to her.

"What is it that you're not saying, Dane?"

As always, she sees right through me.

"We need to leave the country because Stephen is dead," I say, flat and matter of fact.

"What?" Her eyes go wide, and she reels back.

My arms tighten around her, trapping her.

"He tried to rape you," I growl. "I saved you."

"And you..." She swallows hard. "You killed him?"

"Yes. He can never hurt you like that again."

"No." She tries to pull away again, but I don't allow it.

"It's done, Abigail."

The sooner we can move past this, the better.

"You killed someone, Dane!" she exclaims, as though she can't quite believe it.

"To protect you," I counter roughly.

I don't like the way she's looking at me. Like she doesn't know what I'm capable of.

She hasn't looked at me like that since the day we fucked in the ruined barn in the rain.

"That's worse!" she cries. "That means it's my fault."

"It's *his* fault," I snap. "That bastard drugged you. He was going to rape you. The world is a safer place without him in it. You're safer."

She threads her hands through her hair. "No, no, no."

"It's all right." I try to soothe her, but she cringes away from my tender touch.

My heart shreds into bloody ribbons.

"Let me go," she moans. "Let me go, Dane!"

I grasp her closer. "I can't."

A sharp knock on the penthouse door shatters the awful moment. I want to ignore it. I don't want to put an inch of space between my body and hers.

Another knock, harder this time. "North Yorkshire Police."

Fuck.

How are they here already? What clue did I leave behind that would so obviously lead to me?

I smooth my hair into a neater style and climb off the bed. I'm already dressed, ready to head to London the moment Abigail was prepared.

I can deal with the police. I just have to remember how to put on my charming mask.

They have nothing concrete connecting me to the crime. They can't.

Even if they did have forensic evidence that raised suspicion, there's no way it's been processed this quickly.

I take a breath, summon up an expression of confusion and mild concern, then open the door.

"What's this about?" I ask, affable but bewildered.

The uniformed woman peers past me, looking for something. Or someone.

"Is Abigail Foster here?" she asks, her voice clipped and official.

Abigail.

Why would they want to talk to her?

"I'm here," she says from behind me, and I bite back a curse. "What do you need?"

For a moment, fear swamps me. She's going to turn me in. She's going to tell them that I killed Stephen.

But she doesn't say anything else. She steps up beside me and takes my hand in hers, just like when she defended me in front of my family.

I stare down at her with open awe.

She's frightened of my murderous capabilities, but she's still standing by me. She's still choosing me.

"Abigail Foster, you are under arrest on suspicion of the murder of Stephen Lansing."

"No!" I bark, angling my body between the officer and Abigail.

There's another officer at the end of the hall. He

fixes me with a grim stare and comes to join his partner.

"Step aside," he warns me.

Horror crashes down on me, heavy enough that my knees threaten to buckle.

Abigail was Stephen's last appointment yesterday. There will be a written record of it. The police might've already found some sort of drugs in his office. His time of death will align with the time she was in the gallery.

I killed Stephen to save her, but I condemned her.

"Sir, I need you to step aside. Now," the woman insists.

"I'm the one you want." My voice is cold, utterly unfeeling.

Both officers look at me, and they immediately recognize the face of a predator. I don't try to hide it. I let them see exactly what I am.

"Dane, no!"

Abigail's hand tightens around mine, but I yank free of her weaker hold.

Prison has always been my worst-case scenario, ever since the day I shoved Peter out of the window when I was eleven years old. I've spent my entire life since then avoiding this fate.

I wanted so badly to have Abigail, but I was never worthy of her.

I never will be.

"I killed Stephen Lansing," I announce without an ounce of remorse.

After everything I've done to Abigail, redemption isn't possible. I stalked her and violated her. I kidnapped her and caged her. The least I can do now is walk into a cage of my own to save her.

Thank you for reading *Redemption*! I hope you loved this installment in Dane and Abigail's twisted love story. Their dark romance continues in *Absolution*.

ALSO BY JULIA SYKES

Favorite Malady

Compulsion

Redemption

Absolution

Kings of Ruin

Tainted Obsession

Illicit Obsession

Endless Obsession

King of Ruin: The Complete Trilogy

Lord of Ruin

The Captive Series

Sweet Captivity

Claiming My Sweet Captive

Stealing Beauty

Captive Ever After

Pretty Hostage

Wicked King

Ruthless Savior

Eternally His

Their Captive Bride

In Their Hands

In Their Power

In Their Hearts

The Impossible Series

Impossible

Savior

Rogue

Knight

Mentor

Master

King

A Decadent Christmas (An Impossible Series Christmas Special)

Czar

Crusader

Prey (An Impossible Series Short Story)

Highlander

Decadent Knights (An Impossible Series Short Story)

Centurion

Dex

Hero

Wedding Knight (An Impossible Series Short Story)

Valentines at Dusk (An Impossible Series Short Story)

Nice & Naughty (An Impossible Series Christmas Special)

Dark Lessons

Mafia Ménage Trilogy

Mafia Captive

The Daddy and The Dom

Theirs to Protect

Theirs Forever

Fallen Mafia Prince Trilogy

Fallen Prince

Stolen Princess

Fractured Kingdom

Printed in Dunstable, United Kingdom

64885199R00194